Whispers on Petals

Kenneth Thomas

Published by Kenneth Thomas, 2024.

This is a work of fiction. Similarities to real people, places, or events are entirely coincidental.

WHISPERS ON PETALS

First edition. December 3, 2024.

Copyright © 2024 Kenneth Thomas.

ISBN: 979-8230235934

Written by Kenneth Thomas.

To the hopeless romantics,

To those who believe in the soft, lingering glances, the unspoken words that carry the weight of a thousand promises. To those who dream of love that defies the odds, heals the deepest wounds, and blooms like wildflowers in the most unlikely places.

This is for you—keepers of passion, believers in second chances, and eternal seekers of that breathtaking, soul-stirring connection.

May your hearts always find the whispers on petals and the stories waiting to be written.

With love and endless hope, Kenneth Thomas

Whispers on Petals

By Kenneth Thomas

"In the quiet of a garden, where roses bloom and fade, love whispers secrets to the wind."

A novel of longing, resilience, and love that defies both time and circumstance.

Prologue

The dawn crept softly over Ashcombe Manor, brushing the estate in a delicate palette of lavender and gold. Mist clung to the rolling hills like a lover reluctant to part, and the chill of the morning seeped into the earth, holding the promise of an uncertain day. From the once-proud manor house, the faint scent of roses drifted through open windows, mingling with the damp tang of dew and the quiet hum of bees.

In the garden, the roses reigned supreme. Their blooms climbed trellises and spilled over wrought-iron gates, their petals unfurling in silken whispers of cream and crimson. Yet beneath their beauty lay an aching fragility, each stem weighed heavy with blossoms. For years, the garden had flourished against neglect, mirroring the precarious fate of the family who claimed it.

Lady Evangeline Ashcombe stood among the roses, her hands gloved in white kid leather, cradling a single bloom. At twenty-three, Eva bore the Ashcombe legacy in her regal posture and the sharp planes of her high cheekbones. Her porcelain complexion was touched by the faintest blush, but her eyes held a molten resolve, an intensity that defied the genteel world she was born to inhabit.

The estate had fallen into quiet disrepair under the weight of time and unspoken failures. Its survival now rested on Eva's narrow shoulders, a burden her mother never let her forget. Lord Fairmont, with his wealth and titles, had offered an escape—or so her mother insisted. Yet standing here among the roses, Eva felt only the suffocating pull of duty.

A distant sound of hooves broke the stillness, and Eva turned her gaze to the horizon. Through the veil of mist, a lone rider approached. Captain Nathaniel Grey, the estate manager, had been in their employ for scarcely two months, but his presence had already stirred the air with whispers of change.

Eva watched as he drew nearer, his broad shoulders cutting a commanding silhouette against the pale morning light. Nathaniel dismounted with the ease of a man who had lived his life in motion, his boots crunching softly on the gravel as he made his way toward her.

"Lady Ashcombe," he said, his voice rich and steady, with an undercurrent of something unspoken.

"Captain Grey," she replied, tilting her head in polite acknowledgment. Her tone was neutral, but her fingers tightened around the bloom in her hand. "You're up early."

"The land doesn't wait, my lady," he said, slipping off his gloves and tucking them into his belt. His hands were rough and weathered, marked by scars that spoke of a life lived far from the comfort of English countryside estates. "And neither, it seems, do the roses."

A faint smile tugged at Eva's lips. "And yet they endure," she murmured. "Even when neglected."

Nathaniel's hazel eyes lingered on her, unreadable but not unkind. "Endurance is a gift," he said, his voice quiet. "But not one without cost."

For a moment, Eva met his gaze, and the distance between them—the vast chasm of class, expectation, and unspoken yearning—seemed to dissolve. The scent of roses thickened in the air, heady and bittersweet, wrapping around them like a shared secret.

Then, as if the world itself conspired to remind them of their places, the manor's bell pealed from the house, breaking the spell.

Eva straightened, drawing her composure around her like a shield. "If you'll excuse me, Captain, my mother is calling for breakfast."

Nathaniel inclined his head. "Of course, my lady."

But as she turned to leave, his voice stopped her. "Lady Ashcombe," he called, his tone softer now.

She paused, her gloved hand resting on the iron gate. "Yes?"

"The roses are beautiful," he said, glancing at the blooms. "But they'll need pruning soon. Otherwise, the weight of the flowers will break the branches."

Eva hesitated, his words settling over her like a second skin. "Thank you, Captain," she said at last. "I'll keep that in mind."

As she walked toward the manor, the scent of roses lingered, a haunting reminder of what was fragile and fleeting. Behind her, Nathaniel remained in the garden, his gaze fixed on the place where she had stood.

The morning unfolded, heavy with possibilities and impossibilities alike. And though neither of them could name it yet, the first thread of something unbreakable had begun to weave itself between them, as fragile and enduring as the roses that surrounded them.

Chapter One

The morning sunlight poured through the grand windows of Ashcombe Manor's dining room, splintering into fractured beams that danced across the worn oak table. A silver candelabra, tarnished with neglect, stood in the center, its intricate design a relic of the estate's former glory. Despite the golden light, the room carried the chill of unspoken tension, as heavy as the scent of lavender polish that clung to the air.

Lady Margaret Ashcombe sat at the head of the table, her spine as straight as the rigid lines of her high-collared morning gown. Her lips, painted a severe shade of rose, were pressed into a thin line, a silent reproach that filled the space more thoroughly than words. She held a porcelain teacup in one hand, the other poised delicately on the table, her movements practiced and precise.

"Evangeline," Margaret began, her voice cutting through the quiet. "You've spent an inordinate amount of time in the garden lately. A woman of your standing cannot afford such frivolity."

Across the table, Eva sat with perfect composure, delicately buttering a piece of toast. The edges of her porcelain plate were chipped, a detail her mother had likely overlooked, though Eva's gaze lingered on it as if it were a metaphor for the state of the family itself.

"It is not frivolity, Mother," Eva replied evenly, her tone betraying neither irritation nor deference. "The roses require attention if they are to bloom properly. You've always said they are the pride of Ashcombe."

Margaret's eyes narrowed, her fingers tightening around the teacup. "The roses are ornamental, my dear. Your energies would be better spent ensuring our future is secure. Have you written your acceptance to Lord Fairmont?"

The question hung in the air like a blade suspended over Eva's head. She paused, setting down her knife with deliberate care before meeting her mother's gaze.

"I have not," she said, her voice steady but soft.

Margaret inhaled sharply, the tension in her shoulders visible even beneath the fabric of her gown. "You cannot continue to delay. Sebastian Fairmont is offering you a lifeline—not just for yourself but for this family. Do you think your father's poetry will pay the debts? Or your sister's scribblings?"

At the far end of the table, Lord Henry Ashcombe stirred, his pale blue eyes lifting from the open window where his thoughts seemed to drift perpetually. "What a lovely morning," he murmured, as if unaware of the charged air.

Sophia, seated beside him, was doodling absently on the back of a discarded envelope. Her golden curls shimmered in the sunlight, framing a cherubic face that bore an expression of perpetual amusement. She glanced up at Eva, her blue eyes wide with sympathy.

"I think you'd be miserable with Lord Fairmont," she said with her usual candor, the words slipping out before she seemed to consider their weight.

"Sophia," Margaret snapped, her voice like the crack of a whip. "Your sister's happiness is not the matter at hand. Her duty is."

"Duty," Eva repeated softly, the word sitting on her tongue like ash. Her gaze drifted toward the tall windows, where the garden sprawled in a riot of color, wild and untamed against the muted grays of the manor. In her mind, she was already there, walking among the roses, their thorns biting softly into her gloves, the scent of earth and bloom surrounding her.

When she turned back to Margaret, her voice was calm but resolute. "I will not accept Lord Fairmont's proposal. Not yet."

The silence that followed was deafening. Henry hummed a soft tune under his breath, oblivious to the storm brewing, while Sophia returned to her doodles with renewed fervor.

Margaret's expression hardened, her lips a thin line of disapproval. "Then I suggest you find another way to be useful, Evangeline. Perhaps your Captain Grey can teach you something about tending the land, since you seem so determined to play gardener."

Eva's pulse quickened at the mention of Nathaniel's name, but she held her composure. Rising from her chair, she inclined her head politely. "Excuse me, Mother."

Sophia's eyes followed her as she left the room, wide and questioning, but Margaret did not call her back.

The air in the corridor was cooler, less oppressive. Eva's footsteps echoed softly against the polished marble floor as she made her way toward the garden. The scent of roses met her before she stepped outside, mingling with the crisp tang of freshly turned earth.

The garden stretched before her, vibrant and wild, a stark contrast to the crumbling grandeur of the manor. She followed the familiar path to the eastern edge, her breath evening as the tension from breakfast began to dissipate.

Nathaniel Grey was there, crouched near the base of a trellis. His broad hands moved with precision as he inspected the roots of a climbing rose, his shirt sleeves rolled up to reveal forearms tanned and scarred from years of labor and battle. He didn't look up as she approached, but Eva knew he was aware of her presence.

"My mother suggests I learn from you," Eva said, her voice carrying a faint edge of irony. "Apparently, my time in the garden would be better spent under your instruction."

Nathaniel straightened, wiping his hands on a cloth tucked into his belt. A low chuckle rumbled from his chest, and he regarded her with a faint, crooked smile. "I didn't think you were the sort to take orders so easily, my lady."

Eva folded her arms. "I'm not. But if I'm to face another breakfast like this morning's, I might prefer weeding."

He laughed, the sound warm and unrestrained, and for a moment, the tension between them dissolved into something simpler.

Kneeling beside him, Eva let her skirts brush against the dirt. "Show me, then. What do I need to do?"

Nathaniel hesitated, his hazel eyes searching hers. "You'll ruin your gloves."

Eva looked down at her pristine white gloves and tugged them off without hesitation. "Then I suppose I'll ruin them."

Nathaniel shook his head, a soft smile tugging at his lips. "Very well, my lady." He handed her a pair of shears and guided her hands over a branch. "Cut here, clean and deliberate. The plant will heal stronger if you're precise."

As she worked, the weight in her chest began to lift, replaced by the quiet rhythm of the task and the steady presence of the man beside her.

For the first time that day, she felt as if she could breathe again.

Chapter Two

The village of Ashton-by-the-Fen lay just beyond the Ashcombe estate, nestled like a forgotten gem in the curve of the valley. Its cobblestone streets twisted and wound past whitewashed cottages with thatched roofs, their gardens bursting with wildflowers that tumbled over stone walls. The air was fragrant with the mingling scents of baking bread, fresh hay, and the faint briny tang of the river that snaked through the heart of the village.

Eva rarely ventured into Ashton. To her mother, it was a place beneath their station, visited only for charitable acts or the occasional necessary errand. But today, the quiet rebellion of walking alone to the village felt as exhilarating as a dance performed in defiance of propriety.

Her bonnet shielded her face from the sun, though the fabric of her walking dress clung slightly to her skin in the early afternoon warmth. She kept her stride measured, resisting the urge to glance behind her. No one had followed, though she had left the manor with a clear intent to avoid her mother's disapproving gaze.

As she entered the village square, the lively hum of the market greeted her. Stalls laden with vibrant produce and bolts of fabric lined the streets. Merchants called out their wares, their voices rising above the chatter of villagers bartering and exchanging pleasantries.

Eva paused near a stall offering jars of honey and blocks of golden butter. The merchant—a stout woman with a ruddy face—smiled warmly.

"Lady Ashcombe!" the woman greeted, wiping her hands on her apron. "A rare pleasure to see you in the village. Come for some honey, have you?"

Eva smiled faintly. "Not today, Mrs. Griggs. I was simply taking a walk."

Mrs. Griggs tilted her head, her gaze sharp but not unkind. "You've picked a fine day for it, my lady. Though we don't often see you without your sister or mother."

"I suppose not," Eva replied, sidestepping the implicit curiosity in the woman's tone. She continued down the cobbled lane, her steps light but deliberate.

As she rounded a corner, the rhythmic clang of a hammer on an anvil caught her attention. She paused in front of the smithy, where a boy no older than fourteen worked with fierce concentration. Sparks flew in bursts like fireflies around him as he shaped a glowing horseshoe.

"Mind the curve, Jacob!" a deep voice called from the shadows of the workshop.

A man stepped into the sunlight, tall and broad-shouldered, his shirt sleeves rolled up to reveal powerful forearms streaked with soot. Nathaniel Grey.

Eva's breath caught, though she quickly composed herself. He hadn't seen her yet, his attention focused on the boy's work.

"You've got the strength," Nathaniel said, his voice steady and patient. "Now mind the angle—think of how it fits the horse's hoof, not just the iron."

The boy nodded, sweat dripping down his brow, as he adjusted his grip on the hammer.

Nathaniel stepped closer, his gaze sharp and discerning. "Good. Now again."

Eva took a step forward, the gravel crunching softly beneath her boots. Nathaniel glanced up, his hazel eyes meeting hers with a flicker of surprise before settling into something calmer.

"Lady Ashcombe," he said, inclining his head. "I wasn't expecting to see you here."

Eva tilted her head, a faint smile playing at her lips. "I could say the same, Captain Grey. You seem rather at home."

Nathaniel wiped his hands on a cloth tucked into his belt, his expression unguarded but unreadable. "An old habit. A good forge reminds me of simpler times."

"Do you mean your military service?" she asked, her curiosity slipping through before she could temper it.

Nathaniel hesitated, his gaze shifting briefly to the boy at the anvil before returning to her. "No, my lady. Before that."

Eva opened her mouth to press further, but the boy called out.

"Captain Grey, is this right?" Jacob held up the horseshoe, his young face beaming with pride.

Nathaniel nodded approvingly. "That's the one. Now let it cool before you quench it. No rush—you've earned a break."

Jacob grinned and set the horseshoe aside, wiping his face with his sleeve as he disappeared into the workshop.

"You're good with him," Eva said softly, her voice tinged with admiration.

"He listens," Nathaniel replied, his tone matter-of-fact. "Not everyone does."

There was something in his words, unspoken but heavy, that gave Eva pause. She studied him for a moment, noting the slight tension in his jaw and the way his gaze drifted toward the horizon.

"Do you ever miss it?" she asked.

"Miss what?"

"The life you left behind. Before Ashcombe."

Nathaniel's brow furrowed, and he took a slow breath before answering. "Sometimes. But the past has a way of staying where it belongs. Or so I try to remind myself."

Eva nodded, though her curiosity burned hotter. She wanted to ask more, to uncover the layers he kept hidden behind his stoic demeanor, but the weight of propriety held her back.

Before she could respond, the sound of a familiar voice interrupted them.

"Lady Ashcombe!"

Eva turned to see Lord Fairmont approaching, his tailored coat immaculate despite the dust of the village streets. His smile was polished and confident, a practiced expression that rarely faltered.

"Lord Fairmont," Eva said, her tone cool but polite.

"I didn't expect to find you here," he said, his gaze flicking briefly to Nathaniel. "Ashton is rather... quaint."

"I find it charming," Eva replied evenly. "There's an honesty to it."

"Honesty," Fairmont said, his voice laced with amusement. "A quality not always appreciated, my lady."

Nathaniel stepped back slightly, his posture relaxed but his presence unmistakable. Fairmont's gaze lingered on him for a moment before he turned his attention back to Eva.

"May I escort you back to the manor?" Fairmont asked, offering his arm.

Eva hesitated, glancing at Nathaniel, who remained silent but watchful. Something in her chest tightened, though she couldn't name it.

"Thank you, Lord Fairmont," she said finally, "but I think I'll enjoy the walk alone."

Fairmont's smile faltered, but he recovered quickly. "Of course. Another time, then."

He bowed slightly and turned, his polished boots clicking against the cobblestones as he strode away.

Eva glanced at Nathaniel, whose gaze was fixed on the retreating figure.

"Thank you for your advice," she said softly, though she wasn't certain whether she meant the roses, the garden, or something more.

Nathaniel inclined his head, his expression unreadable. "Anytime, my lady."

As Eva turned and began her walk back to the manor, she couldn't shake the feeling that the quiet distance between them spoke louder than words ever could.

Chapter Three

The late afternoon sun poured through the western windows of the Ashcombe library, painting the room in hues of amber and gold. Dust motes swirled lazily in the light, their gentle dance a stark contrast to the restlessness that churned in Eva's chest. She sat in her favorite corner, a well-worn book of Wordsworth's poetry open on her lap.

She had read the same stanza twice without absorbing the words, her thoughts drifting again and again to the village square. Nathaniel's steady gaze, Lord Fairmont's polished charm—two men as different as the lives they represented.

Eva leaned back in her chair, running her fingers along the cracked leather binding of the book. The scent of old paper and ink filled the air, a familiar balm to her frayed nerves. Yet even the tranquility of the library couldn't quiet the unease that lingered after her conversation with Fairmont.

The sharp creak of the library door startled her, and she looked up to see Sophia slipping into the room, her curls bouncing with each step. She carried a sketchbook tucked under one arm and a conspiratorial grin on her lips.

"I thought I'd find you here," Sophia said, flopping into the armchair opposite Eva with the unselfconscious grace of youth.

"And what mischief have you been up to?" Eva asked, arching an eyebrow.

Sophia grinned wider. "None worth mentioning. But I did hear something rather interesting from Mrs. Griggs."

Eva sighed, closing her book. "Should I even ask?"

Sophia leaned forward, her blue eyes sparkling. "She said you and Captain Grey looked quite cozy in the village square this morning. And that Lord Fairmont looked… less pleased."

"Sophia," Eva said sharply, though the warmth creeping up her neck betrayed her.

"Oh, come now," Sophia teased. "Don't pretend you don't know what people are saying. You've got the dashing estate manager and the polished lord vying for your attention. It's like something out of a novel!"

"It's nothing of the sort," Eva replied, rising from her chair and moving to the tall windows. She stared out at the rose garden below, its vibrant blooms glowing in the golden light.

"Perhaps not yet," Sophia said lightly, flipping open her sketchbook. "But it's certainly entertaining to watch."

Eva turned back to her sister, her expression softening. "You read too many novels, Sophia."

"And you read too many poems," Sophia countered, her pencil scratching against the paper. "Maybe if you spent more time dreaming and less time brooding, you'd admit you find Captain Grey intriguing."

Eva shook her head, though a faint smile tugged at her lips. "You're impossible."

"And you're in denial," Sophia quipped, not looking up from her drawing.

The sisters fell into a companionable silence, broken only by the scratch of Sophia's pencil and the distant chirp of birds outside the window. Eva returned to her chair, but instead of picking up her book, she allowed herself to sink into thought.

Nathaniel was unlike anyone she had ever known—steady, unpretentious, and so deeply rooted in integrity that it unsettled her. He was nothing like the men she'd grown up around, with their polished manners and veiled ambitions. And perhaps that was what made him so impossible to ignore.

Dinner that evening was a muted affair, the kind where every word felt heavy with unspoken tensions. Lady Margaret presided over the table like a general, her sharp gaze darting between Eva and Lord Henry, who appeared lost in his own world as usual.

"You received a letter today," Margaret said, breaking the silence as she set down her wineglass.

"Did I?" Eva replied, though she already knew what her mother meant.

Margaret gave her a pointed look. "From Lord Fairmont. He wishes to call on you tomorrow afternoon."

Eva's knife paused mid-air, the faint scrape of silver on porcelain unnaturally loud in the quiet. She placed it down carefully, meeting her mother's gaze. "And what am I expected to say to him?"

"The only sensible answer," Margaret replied, her tone clipped. "You've already kept him waiting far too long."

"I have given this family my every thought, every decision," Eva said quietly, though her voice carried a steely edge. "But I will not give my hand to a man I do not trust."

The silence that followed was deafening. Even Sophia, who often spoke without restraint, kept her head down, her fork hovering over her plate.

Margaret's lips tightened into a thin line. "You speak as though you have the luxury of choice. This is not about trust, Evangeline. It is about survival. Without Lord Fairmont's support, this estate will fall into ruin. Is that what you want?"

Eva stood, the scrape of her chair breaking the stillness. "I want to believe there is another way."

Margaret's gaze burned into her, but she said nothing as Eva turned and left the room.

The cool night air was a balm to Eva's frayed nerves. She wandered through the garden, the gravel crunching softly beneath her boots as she made her way toward the pavilion. The roses glowed faintly in the moonlight, their petals heavy with dew.

She was not surprised to find Nathaniel there. He stood near the eastern trellis, his hands tucked into his pockets as he gazed up at the sky.

"Do you always haunt the garden at night, Captain Grey?" Eva asked, her voice light but tinged with exhaustion.

Nathaniel turned, his expression softening when he saw her. "Only when it seems to need me, my lady."

Eva approached, her steps unhurried. "And tonight? What do the roses require?"

"Patience," he replied. "And care."

She smiled faintly, the tension in her chest easing slightly. "You seem to believe that applies to most things."

"Most things worth saving," he said, his gaze steady.

For a moment, they stood in silence, the quiet hum of the night wrapping around them like a cloak. Eva studied him, the way his presence seemed to ground her even when her thoughts threatened to spiral.

"Nathaniel," she said softly, his name unfamiliar but oddly comforting on her tongue. "Do you ever wish things were different?"

His jaw tightened, and he looked away, his gaze settling on the horizon. "Every day."

The weight of his words settled over her like a second skin, and for the first time, she felt the full measure of the chasm between them. Yet standing here in the garden, surrounded by the quiet resilience of the roses, she wondered if that chasm was not so insurmountable after all.

Chapter Four

The early morning mist clung to the Ashcombe estate like a shroud, softening the edges of the garden and hills. Eva stood at the window of her room, gazing out at the roses glistening with dew. Her thoughts were heavy, circling endlessly around the tension at dinner the night before, her mother's relentless demands, and Nathaniel's quiet, steadfast presence.

A soft knock at her door pulled her from her reverie.

"Come in," Eva called, her voice tinged with weariness.

The door creaked open, and Sophia peeked inside, her curls still loosely pinned and her cheeks flushed with the eagerness of youth. She carried a tray laden with fresh scones and a small jar of honey.

"I thought you might skip breakfast to sulk," Sophia said with a grin, setting the tray down on a side table. "So I brought provisions."

Eva sighed, a smile tugging at the corners of her lips despite her mood. "You're relentless, you know that?"

"I prefer to think of it as being attentive," Sophia replied, perching on the edge of the bed. "Besides, you seemed… off last night. Even more than usual."

"I'm fine," Eva said automatically, though her tone lacked conviction. She moved to the table and broke off a piece of a scone, spreading honey across its warm surface.

Sophia tilted her head, studying her sister. "It's Fairmont, isn't it? He's coming today?"

Eva nodded, her fingers tightening slightly around the knife. "Mother seems to think I'll fall at his feet and thank him for the privilege of saving our estate."

"Would it be so terrible?" Sophia asked, her tone cautious.

Eva's gaze snapped to her sister, her expression incredulous. "How can you say that?"

"I'm not saying you should marry him," Sophia said quickly. "But... the estate, Eva. It's not just about you or Mother. It's everyone. The staff, the tenants... Ashcombe is more than just a house."

Eva set the knife down, her appetite forgotten. "You think I don't know that?"

Sophia hesitated, her hands twisting in her lap. "I think you do. But I also think you're holding out for something that might not exist."

For a moment, neither of them spoke. Then Sophia stood, her shoulders stiff with discomfort. "I'm sorry. I didn't mean to upset you."

"You didn't," Eva said softly, though her chest ached with unspoken emotions. "Thank you for the scones."

Sophia smiled faintly, brushing a curl from her face. "Just don't let Mother bully you too much, alright?"

With that, she slipped out of the room, leaving Eva alone once more.

By the time Lord Fairmont arrived, the mist had burned away, and the garden was bathed in the soft light of a cloudy afternoon. Eva stood in the drawing room, her emerald green day dress chosen carefully for its simplicity. She wanted no pretense, no suggestion of her mother's intentions in her attire.

Fairmont entered with the confidence of a man who had never been refused. His coat, perfectly tailored, caught the faintest sheen of light as he strode into the room. He bowed slightly, his smile warm and practiced.

"Lady Ashcombe," he said, his voice smooth as honey.

"Lord Fairmont," Eva replied, her tone polite but cool.

"I trust you're well?" he asked, his gaze lingering a moment longer than propriety demanded.

"Well enough, thank you."

There was a pause, the kind of silence that Fairmont filled effortlessly with his cultivated charm.

"The roses are spectacular this time of year," he said, stepping toward the window. "I saw them as I rode up. Quite the metaphor for this place, wouldn't you say? Wild yet enduring."

"They do endure," Eva said softly, her eyes narrowing slightly.

"And yet," Fairmont continued, turning to face her, "even the strongest garden needs a steady hand to guide it. Without care, it can wither, no matter how deep its roots."

Eva folded her hands in front of her, her chin lifting slightly. "Is that why you've come, my lord? To offer your steady hand?"

Fairmont's smile faltered for the briefest moment before settling back into place. "I've come because I admire Ashcombe, my lady. And its mistress."

Eva's pulse quickened, though not with the thrill of flattery. "You admire Ashcombe, or you wish to possess it?"

His gaze darkened, his polished demeanor slipping further. "I admire what Ashcombe represents. Legacy, resilience, beauty. And I wish to preserve it. Surely you see that our union would ensure its survival."

"At what cost?" Eva asked, her voice firmer now.

Fairmont took a step closer, his tone dropping to something quieter, more intimate. "You would have security, comfort, and the esteem of society. I would ensure that no harm ever came to you or your family."

Eva held his gaze, her chest tightening with the weight of his words. She could feel the trap in them, the gilded cage he was offering. "And would you ensure my happiness?"

Fairmont's smile grew taut, his patience fraying. "Happiness, my lady, is often a luxury we cannot afford. What I offer is reality."

Eva stepped back, her hands trembling slightly as she clasped them together. "Reality, my lord, is not enough."

The tension between them was palpable, the air thick with unspoken challenges. Before Fairmont could respond, the sound of a voice at the door broke the spell.

"Lady Ashcombe," Nathaniel said, stepping into the room with an apologetic nod. "Forgive the interruption, but there's an urgent matter that requires your attention."

Eva turned to him, relief flooding through her like a tide. "Of course, Captain Grey. Excuse me, Lord Fairmont."

Fairmont's jaw tightened, but he inclined his head. "We'll continue this discussion another time."

As Nathaniel led Eva out of the room and into the cool air of the corridor, she let out a breath she hadn't realized she was holding.

"You have an uncanny sense of timing, Captain," she said, her voice light but strained.

Nathaniel glanced at her, his hazel eyes steady and unreadable. "It seemed like the right moment to intervene."

"For which I'm grateful," Eva replied, a faint smile breaking through her composure. "Though I suspect my mother will have plenty to say about it later."

"Let her say it," Nathaniel said quietly. "You shouldn't have to face this alone."

The sincerity in his voice caught her off guard, and she stopped walking, turning to face him. "Why do you care so much, Nathaniel?"

He hesitated, his gaze flicking away for a moment before returning to hers. "Because I see what you're fighting for. And because... someone should."

For a moment, the weight of the world seemed to ease, and Eva felt a spark of something she hadn't dared hope for—something that felt a little like courage.

Chapter Five

The Ashcombe estate was alive with preparations for the evening's dinner party. Maids hurried through the corridors with polished silver trays and freshly laundered linens, while the faint hum of conversation from the kitchen carried through the lower floors. Lady Margaret had spent the afternoon overseeing every detail, her sharp instructions ensuring that not even the smallest imperfection escaped notice.

Eva stood at the mirror in her room, her maid fastening the final pearl buttons of her gown. The deep emerald fabric clung to her figure with understated elegance, its lace collar brushing against her neck. She adjusted the thin chain of her locket, tucking it beneath the neckline as the maid stepped back to admire her work.

"You look beautiful, my lady," the maid said, her voice tinged with both admiration and pride.

"Thank you, Mary," Eva replied, her tone polite but distant.

When the door clicked shut behind the maid, Eva turned to the window, her gaze drifting over the garden below. The roses were barely visible in the fading light, their colors muted by the encroaching dusk. She wondered if Nathaniel was still out there, tending to the estate even as the rest of the house busied itself with the evening's affairs.

Her thoughts lingered on him longer than she intended. The way he had stood in the drawing room earlier, steady and composed despite the tension in the air. His quiet strength was something she couldn't ignore, no matter how hard she tried.

A sharp knock at the door startled her.

"Evangeline," her mother's voice called, firm and expectant.

Eva opened the door to find Lady Margaret already turned toward the stairs, her gown a severe shade of violet that accentuated her commanding presence.

"The guests are arriving," Margaret said, not bothering to look back. "I trust you'll behave appropriately this evening. Lord Fairmont will expect your attention."

Eva pressed her lips into a thin line but said nothing as she followed her mother down the grand staircase.

The dining room had been transformed into a display of muted opulence. The fire in the hearth cast a golden glow over the polished silverware and crystal goblets arranged with precision on the long table. The soft hum of polite conversation filled the room as the guests mingled, their laughter and murmurs blending into a symphony of genteel propriety.

Lord Fairmont stood near the fireplace, a glass of brandy in hand. His dark eyes scanned the room with the confidence of a man accustomed to admiration. When his gaze landed on Eva, he straightened, his smile deepening.

"Lady Ashcombe," he said as she approached, bowing slightly. "You look radiant this evening."

"Thank you, my lord," Eva replied, her voice cool but courteous.

"Shall we?" he asked, offering his arm.

Eva hesitated, glancing around the room. Her father was seated near the far end of the table, his expression distant as he thumbed through a book he had brought to the party, oblivious to the social expectations surrounding him. Sophia, meanwhile, stood by the window, whispering animatedly with Clara Worthing, her cheeks flushed with laughter.

Eva placed her hand lightly on Fairmont's arm, allowing him to lead her to the table. As they sat, she caught a glimpse of Nathaniel entering the room through a side door, his presence understated yet impossible to ignore. He exchanged quiet words with the butler before moving to stand at the back of the room, his gaze scanning the crowd.

The dinner began with an air of forced conviviality. Margaret directed the conversation with the precision of a conductor, ensuring that each guest felt included while subtly steering the focus toward Lord Fairmont's virtues.

"And tell me, Lord Fairmont," Margaret said, her tone effusive, "have you always had such a keen interest in estates and land management?"

Fairmont smiled, dabbing at his mouth with his napkin. "It has always been a passion of mine, Lady Ashcombe. There is a unique satisfaction in restoring what time has worn down."

"How noble," Margaret said, casting a pointed glance at Eva.

Eva sipped her wine, her expression unreadable.

"And what of you, Lady Ashcombe?" Fairmont asked, his voice rich with calculated charm. "Do you share your mother's passion for preservation?"

"I share her passion for resilience," Eva replied evenly, setting her glass down. "Though I believe preservation is only meaningful when it allows for growth."

Fairmont arched an eyebrow, his smile tightening. "A poetic sentiment. But growth often requires careful guidance, does it not?"

"Perhaps," Eva said, her tone cool. "Or perhaps it requires freedom."

The tension between them was palpable, drawing the attention of nearby guests. Margaret's lips tightened, but before she could interject, the butler entered the room and whispered something to Nathaniel.

Nathaniel's gaze flicked toward Eva, his expression unreadable. He stepped forward, bowing slightly to Margaret. "Forgive the interruption, Lady Ashcombe, but there is an urgent matter requiring your attention."

Margaret frowned. "What matter could possibly warrant—"

"I'll handle it," Eva said, rising from her seat.

Fairmont's jaw tightened, but he remained silent as Eva followed Nathaniel out of the room.

The corridor was cool and quiet, a stark contrast to the oppressive warmth of the dining room. Nathaniel walked ahead of her, his stride purposeful but unhurried.

"What is it?" Eva asked when they reached the library.

Nathaniel closed the door behind them, turning to face her. "I needed to get you out of there."

Eva blinked, startled by his candor. "Excuse me?"

"Fairmont," he said, his voice low. "I could see how uncomfortable you were. I thought you might need an escape."

Eva stared at him, a rush of emotions swirling in her chest—gratitude, confusion, and something deeper she couldn't quite name. "That's... bold of you, Captain Grey."

He held her gaze, his expression steady. "I didn't mean to overstep."

"You didn't," she said softly. "Thank you."

For a moment, they stood in silence, the weight of unspoken words filling the space between them. The distant hum of voices from the dining room was muffled by the thick oak door, leaving only the faint crackle of the fireplace to break the quiet.

"Nathaniel," Eva began, her voice barely above a whisper, "why do you care so much?"

His jaw tightened, and he looked away, his hands clasped behind his back. "Because you deserve better than him. Better than all of this."

The raw honesty in his voice left her breathless.

"I don't know if that's true," she said, stepping closer.

"It is," he said, his gaze locking onto hers.

Eva felt the pull between them, a force that seemed to defy reason. She took another step closer, her voice trembling. "Nathaniel..."

The sound of footsteps in the corridor broke the moment, and they both stepped back instinctively.

Sophia's voice called out, her tone light but tinged with urgency. "Eva? Are you in here?"

Eva turned toward the door, her heart pounding. "Yes, Sophia. I'm coming."

She glanced back at Nathaniel, his expression unreadable. "Thank you," she said again, her voice quieter now.

He inclined his head, and as she stepped out of the library, she couldn't help but feel that she was leaving a part of herself behind.

Chapter Six

The morning light seeped through the estate's eastern windows, illuminating the long dining table that now felt emptier than ever. Breakfast had been an exercise in silence; Lady Margaret had scarcely looked at Eva, her disapproval manifesting in clipped instructions to the staff and the faint but unmistakable press of her lips into a thin line.

Eva had excused herself early, leaving behind her untouched tea and a growing sense of unease. She walked the length of the great hall, her footsteps echoing against the marble floor as she made her way toward the garden.

Outside, the roses greeted her with their usual quiet resilience. She knelt beside a trellis, her fingers brushing over the dew-damp leaves. The earthy scent of the garden grounded her, offering a fleeting reprieve from the weight of expectations pressing on her chest.

Her thoughts drifted to Nathaniel—his quiet strength, his unexpected candor. The memory of their exchange in the library lingered, an unspoken truth that unsettled and thrilled her in equal measure. She shook her head, as if to rid herself of the thought, and turned her attention back to the roses.

"You'll ruin your dress kneeling like that."

The voice startled her, and she looked up to see Nathaniel standing a few paces away, his arms crossed and a faint smile tugging at his lips.

"Good morning to you too, Captain Grey," Eva said, rising to her feet and brushing her hands against her skirts.

He stepped closer, his boots crunching softly on the gravel path. "I didn't mean to intrude. You just seemed... deep in thought."

"I often am when I'm out here," she replied, her tone lighter than she felt. "The garden has a way of clearing my mind."

Nathaniel nodded, his gaze sweeping over the roses. "It's peaceful. A rarity these days."

"Indeed," Eva murmured. She hesitated, then added, "Thank you for last night."

Nathaniel glanced at her, his hazel eyes steady. "You don't need to thank me."

"I do," Eva insisted. "If you hadn't intervened..." She trailed off, the memory of Fairmont's veiled insistence making her stomach twist.

Nathaniel's jaw tightened. "He oversteps. Always has."

Eva's brow furrowed. "You've known him long?"

Nathaniel hesitated, his gaze shifting to the horizon. "Long enough to know his kind."

There was a weight to his words that made Eva pause. "What do you mean?"

He exhaled slowly, his shoulders stiffening. "Men like him... they see the world as something to be acquired, conquered. People, places—they're all just pieces in their game. Fairmont's no different."

Eva studied him, the tension in his frame speaking volumes. "And you? What do you see?"

Nathaniel's eyes met hers, a flicker of vulnerability breaking through his composed exterior. "I see people who deserve more than they're given. Places that deserve to thrive, not just survive."

Eva's chest tightened, his words resonating more deeply than she cared to admit.

Before she could respond, the faint sound of footsteps approached, and Sophia appeared at the edge of the garden, her cheeks flushed from the cool morning air.

"There you are!" she called, her tone bright. "I've been looking for you everywhere."

Eva turned, a faint smile softening her expression. "Is something wrong?"

"Not at all," Sophia replied, though her gaze flicked curiously to Nathaniel. "I just wanted to tell you that Mrs. Griggs is in the kitchen with the most scandalous bit of gossip. Apparently, someone spotted Lord Fairmont and Miss Worthing riding together this morning."

Eva's brow arched. "Miss Worthing? Clara?"

"The very same," Sophia said with a grin. "And if Mrs. Griggs is to be believed, they looked rather... cozy."

Eva couldn't help the faint laugh that escaped her lips. "Well, I suppose even Lord Fairmont isn't immune to a bit of intrigue."

Sophia laughed, then gave Nathaniel a quick curtsy. "Good morning, Captain Grey. Don't let my sister keep you from your duties."

Nathaniel inclined his head, a faint smile tugging at his lips. "Good morning, Miss Sophia."

As Sophia disappeared back toward the house, Eva turned back to Nathaniel, the momentary levity fading. "Do you think it's true?" she asked softly.

Nathaniel shrugged. "Perhaps. But men like Fairmont rarely limit their ambitions to just one path."

Eva frowned, his words stirring a quiet unease.

"Be careful," Nathaniel said after a moment, his tone low. "He won't give up easily."

"I can handle him," Eva replied, though her voice lacked its usual certainty.

Nathaniel stepped closer, his gaze steady and unyielding. "You shouldn't have to."

Eva's breath caught, the quiet intensity of his presence enveloping her. For a moment, the world seemed to still, the distant hum of the estate fading into nothingness.

"Thank you," she said again, her voice barely above a whisper.

Nathaniel nodded, his expression softening. "Always."

The rest of the day passed in a blur of routine tasks and polite distractions, but the quiet moment in the garden lingered in Eva's mind. By the time the sun dipped below the horizon, casting the estate in hues of pink and orange, she found herself drawn back to the garden, its solitude a balm to her restless thoughts.

She wandered the paths aimlessly, her fingers brushing against the petals of the roses. Their beauty was fleeting, delicate, yet impossibly enduring.

The sound of footsteps broke the stillness, and she turned to see Nathaniel approaching once more.

"Still here?" he asked, his voice carrying the faintest trace of amusement.

"And you?" Eva countered, a small smile tugging at her lips.

He shrugged. "I couldn't sleep."

They stood in silence for a moment, the weight of the day settling between them.

"Nathaniel," Eva began softly, her gaze fixed on the roses. "Do you ever feel as though you're caught between two worlds? One that demands everything of you and one that offers nothing in return?"

Nathaniel's brow furrowed, and he stepped closer. "All the time."

Eva turned to him, her eyes searching his. "What do you do?"

He hesitated, his gaze steady. "I fight for the world that matters. Even when it feels like I'll lose."

His words struck a chord deep within her, and for the first time in a long while, Eva felt a glimmer of clarity.

"You make it sound so simple," she said, a faint smile breaking through her melancholy.

"It's not," Nathaniel replied, his voice low. "But some things are worth the fight."

As the last light of day faded from the sky, Eva couldn't help but wonder if she was one of those things.

Chapter Seven

The days following Lord Fairmont's visit were marked by a strange quietness in the household. Lady Margaret, though outwardly calm, carried an air of tightly wound tension, her clipped instructions to the staff and pointed silences aimed at Eva speaking volumes. Eva, for her part, had withdrawn into herself, spending hours in the garden or taking long walks along the edges of the estate.

Her thoughts returned repeatedly to the garden moments with Nathaniel, the quiet intensity of his words, and the unspoken weight of the connection they both seemed to avoid acknowledging. She found herself searching for him more often—on the paths, near the stables, anywhere his work might take him. Yet when they crossed paths, she hesitated, unsure of what to say or how to bridge the growing tension between them.

The morning was crisp, with a chill in the air that hinted at the coming autumn. Eva had taken her sketchbook to the farthest edge of the estate, where the land sloped down toward the river. The water was clear and cold, its surface catching the sunlight in dazzling flashes.

She perched on a fallen log, her skirts spread carefully to avoid the damp moss, and began to sketch the scene before her. The act of drawing steadied her, pulling her focus away from her racing thoughts.

A rustle in the nearby brush startled her, and she turned to see Nathaniel emerging from the trees, his jacket slung over one shoulder and a loose strand of dark hair falling across his brow.

"You're far from the house," he remarked, his voice carrying easily over the quiet murmur of the river.

"As are you," Eva replied, setting down her pencil.

Nathaniel walked closer, his boots crunching softly against the leaf-strewn ground. "I was inspecting the eastern boundary. There's a patch of fencing that needs repair."

Eva smiled faintly. "Always working, Captain Grey."

"Someone has to," he said with a touch of humor, though his gaze lingered on her with quiet concern. "And you? Are you escaping something, or just looking for solitude?"

"Both," she admitted, gesturing toward the sketchbook. "I needed a change of scenery."

Nathaniel glanced at the sketchbook, his brow arching slightly. "May I?"

Eva hesitated, then handed it to him. He flipped through the pages carefully, his expression softening as he studied her drawings.

"You've captured the garden beautifully," he said, pausing on a sketch of the roses near the trellis. "And the estate. It's... alive in your work."

"Thank you," Eva said quietly, her chest tightening at the unexpected compliment.

Nathaniel handed the sketchbook back, his gaze meeting hers. "Why do you hide this? Your talent deserves to be seen."

Eva shook her head, tucking the sketchbook under her arm. "It's just a pastime, nothing more."

"Maybe it's more than that," Nathaniel said, his tone gentle but firm.

Their eyes met, the weight of his words lingering between them. For a moment, Eva felt as though he could see through her carefully constructed defenses, straight to the heart of her doubts and dreams.

She looked away, her fingers tightening around the sketchbook. "I doubt my mother would see it that way."

"Your mother sees the world through narrow windows," Nathaniel said, his voice edged with quiet frustration. "That doesn't mean you have to."

Eva opened her mouth to respond, but the sound of distant voices carried through the trees, breaking the moment. She turned to see a pair of figures on horseback approaching along the path—a maid from the manor and, to her dismay, Lord Fairmont.

Fairmont dismounted gracefully, his polished boots barely stirring the dust as he approached. His smile was warm but tightly controlled, his gaze flicking between Eva and Nathaniel.

"Lady Ashcombe," he said smoothly. "What a pleasant surprise."

"Lord Fairmont," Eva replied, her tone cool.

Fairmont's smile widened, though his eyes lingered on Nathaniel for a fraction too long. "And Captain Grey. How fortunate to find you both here. I've come to discuss the improvements to the estate's eastern acreage."

Nathaniel inclined his head, his expression unreadable. "I was just inspecting the boundary fencing."

"Excellent," Fairmont said, his tone oozing approval. "Perhaps we can review it together."

The tension between the two men was palpable, though neither raised their voice or betrayed their emotions openly. Eva stepped forward, her gaze steady. "I'm sure Captain Grey has the situation well in hand, my lord. Perhaps you'd like to return to the manor for refreshments?"

Fairmont hesitated, his expression tightening briefly before he recovered. "Of course. But do join me soon, Lady Ashcombe. We have much to discuss."

With a final, lingering glance at Nathaniel, he turned and mounted his horse. The maid followed, and the sound of hoofbeats faded into the distance.

Nathaniel exhaled softly, his jaw tight. "He's persistent, I'll give him that."

"Too persistent," Eva muttered, her hands trembling slightly.

Nathaniel stepped closer, his gaze softening. "If he's pushing you too far—"

"I can handle him," Eva said quickly, though the words felt hollow.

Nathaniel studied her for a moment, his hazel eyes searching hers. "You shouldn't have to handle this alone."

"I don't have a choice," she said, her voice tinged with frustration. "My mother—"

"Your mother doesn't define you," Nathaniel said sharply, his voice cutting through her protests. "You have a choice, Eva. Don't let anyone take that from you."

The intensity in his voice left her momentarily speechless. She turned away, her gaze drifting toward the river. "Sometimes it feels like the choice is already made for me."

Nathaniel stepped closer, his voice softer now. "Then make a new one. For yourself."

Eva turned back to him, her chest tight with a mix of fear and hope. "You make it sound so simple."

"It's not," Nathaniel said, his gaze steady. "But it's worth it."

For a moment, the world seemed to fade away, leaving only the sound of the river and the quiet strength of his presence. Eva took a slow breath, the weight on her chest lifting slightly.

"Thank you," she said softly.

Nathaniel nodded, his expression unreadable. "Always."

Chapter Eight

The Ashcombe estate felt heavier that evening, its silence marked by the absence of the usual hum of activity. Dinner had been tense, with Lady Margaret's disapproval hanging thick in the air. Even Sophia, who often filled the room with her chatter, had been unusually subdued, casting worried glances at Eva throughout the meal.

Eva had barely touched her food. Her thoughts were a jumble of emotions—Fairmont's persistence, Nathaniel's quiet insistence that she fight for herself, and the growing realization that she could no longer ignore the battle raging within her.

After dinner, she excused herself early, retreating to the library where the low-burning fire offered a semblance of comfort. The room smelled faintly of wood smoke and aged leather, the familiar scents wrapping around her like a cocoon.

She sank into her favorite chair by the fire, a cup of tea cooling on the table beside her. The words on the page of the book she'd opened blurred together, her mind too restless to focus. She set the book aside, letting her head fall back against the chair, her gaze drifting to the intricate carvings on the ceiling.

The knock at the door was soft, hesitant.

"Come in," she called, sitting up straighter.

The door opened to reveal Sophia, her golden curls falling loose around her shoulders. She stepped inside, her expression a mix of curiosity and concern.

"You've been avoiding everyone all evening," Sophia said, closing the door behind her.

"I needed some time to think," Eva replied, gesturing to the empty chair across from her.

Sophia sat, tucking her legs beneath her and wrapping her arms around herself. "About Fairmont?"

Eva hesitated, then nodded. "Among other things."

Sophia tilted her head, her blue eyes sharp despite her usual lighthearted demeanor. "You don't trust him, do you?"

"No," Eva admitted, her voice barely above a whisper.

Sophia leaned forward, her expression earnest. "Then don't let Mother force you into this. You have more courage than you think, Eva. You always have."

Eva smiled faintly, reaching out to take her sister's hand. "You've always had too much faith in me."

Sophia shook her head, her curls bouncing. "Not faith—belief. There's a difference."

They sat in silence for a moment, the crackle of the fire filling the space between them.

"Do you think Father would understand?" Eva asked quietly.

Sophia hesitated, her gaze dropping to their joined hands. "Father lives in his own world most of the time. But I think, deep down, he'd want you to be happy. Even if he can't say it."

Eva nodded, her throat tightening.

"And Nathaniel?" Sophia asked, her voice dropping to a conspiratorial whisper.

Eva's cheeks flushed, and she looked away. "What about him?"

"Oh, don't play coy," Sophia teased, her grin returning. "I've seen the way you look at him. And the way he looks at you."

"Sophia," Eva warned, though her tone lacked its usual firmness.

"I'm just saying," Sophia said, holding up her hands in mock surrender. "You deserve someone who sees you for who you are, not what you represent. And I think he does."

Eva's chest tightened, her sister's words cutting through her defenses with startling accuracy.

"Goodnight, Sophia," she said, rising from her chair.

Sophia smiled knowingly, standing as well. "Goodnight, Eva. Just... think about what I said, will you?"

Eva nodded, watching as her sister slipped out of the room.

Later that night, unable to sleep, Eva found herself wandering the halls of the manor. The dimly lit corridors stretched before her, the flickering light of the sconces casting shadows that danced along the walls.

Her feet carried her toward the garden almost unconsciously, drawn to its quiet solace. The cool night air wrapped around her as she stepped outside, the scent of roses faint but comforting.

Nathaniel was there, as she somehow knew he would be. He stood near the eastern trellis, his hands tucked into his pockets and his gaze fixed on the darkened horizon.

"You're always here when I need you," Eva said softly, her voice carrying across the stillness.

Nathaniel turned, his expression softening when he saw her. "And yet you always seem surprised."

She smiled faintly, stepping closer. "Perhaps I shouldn't be."

They stood in silence for a moment, the moonlight casting a silvery glow over the garden. The tension that had followed Eva all evening seemed to ease in Nathaniel's presence, his quiet strength grounding her in a way she couldn't fully explain.

"I'm leaving tomorrow," Nathaniel said suddenly, his voice breaking the silence.

Eva's heart lurched. "Leaving?"

"Just for a day," he clarified. "There's a meeting in the village about the estate's finances. It might offer a way to ease some of the pressure on Ashcombe."

She nodded, relief washing over her, though it was quickly followed by a pang of guilt. "You always seem to think of everything."

"Not everything," he said quietly, his gaze fixed on her.

The weight of his words settled over her, and she took a slow breath. "Nathaniel, I…"

She hesitated, the words catching in her throat.

"You don't have to say anything," he said, his voice gentle. "But whatever happens, know that you have a choice, Eva. You always have."

Her chest tightened, the intensity of his gaze making it impossible to look away. For a moment, the world seemed to fall away, leaving only the quiet hum of the night and the unspoken connection between them.

"Thank you," she said softly, her voice trembling.

Nathaniel nodded, his expression unreadable. "Goodnight, my lady."

"Goodnight, Nathaniel," she whispered, watching as he disappeared into the shadows of the garden.

As she turned back toward the manor, her heart felt heavier than ever, weighed down by the choices she knew she had to make—and the consequences she could no longer avoid.

Chapter Nine

The village of Ashton-by-the-Fen bustled with activity as Eva arrived in the early afternoon. The cobblestone streets were lined with carts and stalls, their bright displays of produce and textiles creating a tapestry of life against the muted tones of the thatched cottages. Children darted between the market stalls, their laughter ringing out over the chatter of merchants and buyers.

Eva's carriage pulled to a stop near the edge of the square, and she stepped out, brushing her gloved hands against her skirts as she glanced around. She hadn't planned to come to the village that day, but after a restless morning at Ashcombe, the thought of lingering within the estate's walls had been unbearable.

She made her way toward the market, her movements careful and deliberate as she navigated the crowd. The villagers greeted her with polite nods, their curiosity evident but restrained. She paused by a stall selling jars of honey and loaves of freshly baked bread, the scent of warm crusts mingling with the crisp autumn air.

"Lady Ashcombe," a familiar voice called from behind her.

Eva turned to see Mrs. Griggs, the stout, cheerful merchant who seemed to know every bit of gossip in Ashton. She held a basket filled with herbs and flowers, her round face alight with a warm smile.

"Mrs. Griggs," Eva said, returning the smile. "How are you this afternoon?"

"Oh, as busy as ever," Mrs. Griggs replied. "And what brings you to the village today, my lady? It's not often we see you here alone."

"I needed a change of scenery," Eva said lightly, though she could tell Mrs. Griggs wasn't entirely convinced.

"Well, you've picked a lively day for it," the merchant said with a knowing twinkle in her eye. "Though I hear Captain Grey's down at the meeting hall. Likely to be there a while, what with all the chatter about the new agreements."

Eva's heart quickened at the mention of Nathaniel. "Agreements?" she asked, keeping her tone casual.

"Something to do with the land and tenancy," Mrs. Griggs said, lowering her voice conspiratorially. "I heard Lord Fairmont's been stirring the pot, trying to sway the council to his way of thinking."

Eva's chest tightened. "Lord Fairmont is involved?"

"Oh, yes," Mrs. Griggs said with a nod. "He's been meeting with some of the bigger landowners, saying there's a chance to modernize the village—whatever that means. Not everyone's happy about it, though."

Eva frowned, a knot of unease forming in her stomach. "Thank you, Mrs. Griggs. I think I'll take a walk toward the hall."

"Of course, my lady," Mrs. Griggs said, her smile fading slightly as she watched Eva turn and walk away.

The meeting hall stood at the edge of the square, its weathered stone facade and arched windows giving it a solemn, imposing presence. Eva approached quietly, her footsteps muffled by the packed dirt of the path.

The sound of voices reached her before she entered, their tones ranging from low murmurs to raised arguments. She hesitated by the door, unsure whether to interrupt, but a familiar voice cut through the din, firm and resolute.

"Fairmont's proposal may promise progress, but it comes at a cost," Nathaniel said, his words clear and measured. "The tenants would lose their independence, their livelihoods tied to the whims of men who see them as little more than figures in a ledger."

"And what do you propose, Captain Grey?" another voice countered, sharp with skepticism. "We can't ignore the state of the land forever. It's failing."

"There are other ways to modernize," Nathaniel replied. "Methods that don't strip the villagers of their dignity or their ability to make a living."

Eva stepped into the hall quietly, her presence unnoticed at first as the debate continued. Nathaniel stood at the center of the room, his sleeves rolled up and his expression calm but determined. Around him, a mix of villagers and landowners listened with varying degrees of interest and dissent.

At the far end of the room, Lord Fairmont leaned casually against a wooden pillar, his arms crossed and a faint smirk playing on his lips. His gaze flicked toward Eva as she entered, and his smirk deepened.

"Ah, Lady Ashcombe," Fairmont said smoothly, his voice cutting through the conversation. "What an unexpected pleasure."

All eyes turned to her, and Eva straightened, forcing a calm smile. "Good afternoon, Lord Fairmont. Captain Grey."

Nathaniel's gaze met hers, a flicker of surprise crossing his face before he inclined his head. "Lady Ashcombe."

"I didn't mean to interrupt," she said, stepping further into the room. "But I couldn't help overhearing."

"Then perhaps you can offer your opinion," Fairmont said, his tone laced with amusement. "Surely you must have thoughts on how best to secure Ashcombe's future."

Eva's pulse quickened, but she refused to let her composure falter. "I believe the future should be built on respect and cooperation, not coercion."

Fairmont's smirk faltered slightly, but he recovered quickly. "A noble sentiment, my lady. But progress often requires difficult decisions."

"True," Eva replied evenly. "But those decisions should not come at the expense of those who depend on us."

A murmur of agreement rippled through the room, and Nathaniel's expression softened, a hint of pride in his eyes.

Fairmont straightened, his tone growing colder. "And who will bear the cost of this noble ideal, Lady Ashcombe? Your family? Your tenants? Or perhaps Captain Grey?"

The question hung in the air, a challenge meant to unsettle her. But Eva met his gaze unflinchingly. "We will all bear it together. That is what it means to be a part of something greater than ourselves."

The room fell silent, the weight of her words settling over the crowd. Even Fairmont seemed momentarily at a loss for a reply.

Nathaniel stepped forward, his voice steady and resolute. "Lady Ashcombe is right. This estate, this village, is more than numbers and profits. It's a community. And that's worth fighting for."

A murmur of agreement rose again, louder this time, and Fairmont's expression darkened.

Eva turned to Nathaniel, her heart swelling with gratitude. "Thank you, Captain Grey," she said softly, her voice carrying across the room.

He inclined his head, his gaze holding hers for a moment longer than necessary.

As the meeting broke up and the crowd began to disperse, Fairmont approached her, his smile tight and forced. "You play a dangerous game, my lady."

"It's not a game," Eva said, her voice calm but firm. "It's a choice."

Fairmont's eyes narrowed, but he said nothing more, turning and striding out of the hall.

Nathaniel appeared at her side, his presence a quiet comfort. "That was brave," he said softly.

"It felt necessary," Eva replied, her voice trembling slightly.

He smiled faintly, his gaze warm. "Sometimes the right choice is."

As they stepped out into the fading sunlight, Eva felt a strange sense of clarity settle over her. For the first time, she knew she was no longer just reacting to the forces around her. She was choosing her path—and it was one she would walk with purpose.

Chapter Ten

The ride back to Ashcombe Manor was silent, the carriage jolting softly over the uneven roads as the sun dipped below the horizon. Eva gazed out of the window, her thoughts tumbling over one another in an endless stream. The confrontation with Fairmont, the quiet strength of Nathaniel's support, and the murmured approval of the villagers—it all lingered in her mind, weaving a tapestry of doubt, resolve, and a faint spark of hope.

By the time the manor came into view, bathed in the last light of dusk, Eva felt the weight of the day settle on her shoulders. She climbed the steps to the front door, her footsteps faltering as she reached the threshold. Taking a steadying breath, she pushed the door open and stepped inside.

The entryway was dimly lit, the faint hum of activity from the kitchens the only sound breaking the silence. Eva handed her gloves and bonnet to the waiting maid, then made her way toward the drawing room, where she knew her mother would be waiting.

Lady Margaret was seated in her usual chair, her posture stiff and regal, a cup of tea balanced delicately in her hands. She looked up as Eva entered, her sharp gaze narrowing slightly.

"You've been gone all afternoon," Margaret said, her tone cold.

"I went to the village," Eva replied evenly, taking a seat across from her.

"To the village?" Margaret set her teacup down with a faint clatter. "For what purpose?"

"There was a meeting regarding the estate and its tenants," Eva said. "I thought it important to hear their concerns."

Margaret's lips pressed into a thin line. "And I suppose Captain Grey encouraged this... excursion?"

Eva met her mother's gaze, her voice calm but firm. "Nathaniel had no part in my decision. It was my own."

Her mother's expression hardened. "Evangeline, you must understand that these matters are far beyond your scope. Your place is here, ensuring this family's survival—not meddling in the affairs of tenants and laborers."

Eva's jaw tightened, her hands curling into fists in her lap. "Those tenants and laborers are the foundation of this estate. If we ignore their struggles, there will be nothing left to survive."

Margaret's eyes flashed with anger. "Do not presume to lecture me on duty, Evangeline. I have spent my life ensuring this family's survival while you flit about the garden or waste your time in the village."

"I am trying to do what is right," Eva said, her voice rising. "Not just for this family, but for everyone who depends on us."

Margaret rose abruptly, her chair scraping against the floor. "Enough," she said sharply. "You will stop this nonsense immediately. Lord Fairmont is offering us a lifeline, and you will not throw it away because of some misplaced sense of idealism."

Eva stood as well, her heart pounding in her chest. "I will not marry Lord Fairmont."

The words hung in the air, heavy and unyielding. Margaret stared at her, stunned into silence for a moment.

"You are being reckless," Margaret said finally, her voice trembling with barely restrained fury. "You would jeopardize everything for what? Some childish notion of independence?"

"For the chance to choose my own future," Eva said, her voice steady despite the storm raging inside her. "I will not be a pawn in anyone's game—not yours, not Fairmont's."

Margaret's hand trembled as she pointed toward the door. "Go to your room, Evangeline. I will not speak of this again tonight."

Eva hesitated, her throat tightening with emotion. "I'm sorry, Mother," she said softly. "But this is my decision."

She turned and left the room, her footsteps echoing in the silent corridor.

The garden was dark and quiet, the cool night air brushing against Eva's skin as she wandered the paths. Her mind was a whirlwind of thoughts, her mother's harsh words ringing in her ears. She wrapped her arms around herself, seeking comfort in the familiar scent of roses.

"Eva."

The sound of Nathaniel's voice startled her, and she turned to see him standing near the trellis, his figure barely visible in the moonlight.

"What are you doing out here?" she asked, her voice trembling.

"I might ask you the same," he said, stepping closer.

Eva looked away, her eyes stinging with unshed tears. "I needed air. And silence."

Nathaniel studied her for a moment, his brow furrowed. "Your mother?"

Eva nodded, unable to speak.

Nathaniel sighed softly, his expression pained. "She doesn't see what you're trying to do, does she?"

"She sees what she wants to see," Eva said bitterly. "To her, I'm a means to an end."

Nathaniel stepped closer, his presence steady and grounding. "You're more than that, Eva. You know you are."

Her gaze lifted to meet his, her chest tightening at the quiet intensity in his eyes. "I don't know what I am anymore."

Nathaniel's hand reached out, hesitating for a moment before brushing lightly against her arm. "You're brave. And kind. And stronger than you realize."

Eva's breath caught, the warmth of his touch seeping through her sleeve. "Nathaniel…"

He stepped back slightly, his jaw tightening. "I should go. It's late."

But before he could turn, Eva reached for his hand, stopping him. "Don't," she said softly.

Nathaniel froze, his gaze locking onto hers. The distance between them seemed to shrink, the world around them fading into nothing.

"I don't know what to do," Eva whispered, her voice trembling.

"You don't have to figure it out alone," Nathaniel said, his voice low and steady. "I'll be here. No matter what."

The weight of his words settled over her, and for the first time in days, Eva felt a glimmer of hope.

"Thank you," she said softly, her fingers tightening around his.

Nathaniel nodded, his gaze unwavering. "Always."

As they stood together in the moonlit garden, Eva felt a quiet strength begin to build within her—a strength that told her she was not as alone as she'd feared.

Chapter Eleven

The next morning, the tension in the manor was palpable. Lady Margaret had taken her breakfast in her private sitting room, an unspoken declaration of her displeasure. Sophia tiptoed around the house with uncharacteristic quiet, her usually cheerful presence muted by the weight of the previous night's confrontation.

Eva sat in the morning room, a pot of tea cooling on the table before her. The sunlight streaming through the tall windows did little to lift her spirits, her thoughts circling endlessly around the argument with her mother. She had expected resistance, but the sheer force of Margaret's anger had left her shaken.

The sound of boots against the polished floor broke through her reverie. She looked up to see Nathaniel standing in the doorway, his posture relaxed but his expression carefully guarded.

"Good morning, Lady Ashcombe," he said, inclining his head.

Eva managed a faint smile. "Good morning, Captain Grey. What brings you here?"

"There's something I thought you should see," Nathaniel replied, stepping into the room. "If you're free."

Eva hesitated for only a moment before standing. "I could use a distraction."

Nathaniel led her to the stables, where a small group of horses were being saddled by the stable hands. One, a dark bay mare with a sleek coat, nickered softly as Nathaniel approached.

"I thought a ride might do you some good," Nathaniel said, his tone light but his gaze serious.

Eva looked at the mare, then back at Nathaniel. "I didn't realize you were in the habit of arranging outings for distraught ladies."

His lips twitched in a faint smile. "Only for those who need it most."

A warmth spread through her chest, and she stepped forward, allowing Nathaniel to help her mount. His hands were firm and steady as he guided her, his touch lingering just a moment longer than necessary.

Once they were both astride their horses, Nathaniel led the way toward the edge of the estate. The morning air was crisp, carrying the faint scent of pine and earth as they rode along a winding path bordered by trees. The rhythmic sound of hooves against the ground was soothing, a welcome reprieve from the turmoil in Eva's mind.

After some time, Nathaniel slowed his horse, glancing back at her. "There's a place I think you'll like. It's not far."

Eva nodded, curiosity stirring within her. "Lead the way."

The path opened onto a small clearing, where the land sloped gently down to a stream that glimmered in the sunlight. Wildflowers swayed in the breeze, their colors vibrant against the lush green of the grass.

Eva dismounted, her boots sinking slightly into the soft earth as she stepped closer to the stream. The sound of the water rushing over smooth stones filled the air, its gentle rhythm calming.

"It's beautiful," she said softly, turning to Nathaniel.

He had dismounted as well, his horse grazing nearby as he stood a few paces away, his hands resting lightly on his hips. "I thought you might like it. It's a good place to think."

Eva smiled faintly, her gaze drifting back to the stream. "You seem to know what I need better than I do."

Nathaniel's expression softened. "Perhaps I just know what it's like to feel trapped."

Her breath hitched, his words cutting through her like a blade. "Do you still feel that way?"

"Sometimes," he admitted, his voice low. "But being here, working with the land, with the people—it helps. It reminds me there's something worth fighting for."

Eva turned to him fully, her chest tightening. "And what about you, Nathaniel? What do you fight for?"

His hazel eyes met hers, unguarded and filled with an intensity that made her heart race. "For those who can't. For those who deserve more than they've been given."

The air between them seemed to thrum with unspoken emotion, the distant sound of the stream fading into the background. Eva took a slow step toward him, her gaze never leaving his.

"Nathaniel," she began, her voice trembling slightly, "I don't know if I can do this. The weight of it all—it feels impossible."

His expression softened further, and he reached out, his hand brushing lightly against her arm. "You can, Eva. You're stronger than you think."

Her breath caught, the warmth of his touch grounding her even as her thoughts spun wildly. "How can you be so sure?"

"Because I've seen it," he said simply.

The truth in his words left her speechless, and for a moment, they stood in silence, the world around them seeming to hold its breath.

"I should go back," Eva said finally, her voice quiet.

Nathaniel nodded, stepping back. "I'll ride with you."

The ride back to the manor was quiet, the tension between them unspoken but palpable. By the time they reached the stables, the sun was high in the sky, casting the estate in a golden glow.

Nathaniel helped her dismount, his hands steady as they guided her to the ground. For a moment, they stood close, the warmth of his presence seeping into her.

"Thank you," Eva said softly, her voice barely above a whisper.

Nathaniel nodded, his gaze lingering on hers. "Always."

As she walked back toward the manor, Eva felt a strange mixture of resolve and uncertainty stirring within her. Nathaniel's words, his unwavering belief in her, had struck something deep within her—a spark she could no longer ignore.

Chapter Twelve

The manor hummed with an unnatural quiet when Eva returned, her steps echoing softly against the polished marble floor. She paused in the entryway, her gaze drifting to the grand staircase that loomed before her. Every step back into the house felt heavier than the last, as though the weight of her responsibilities clung to her like a shadow.

"Evangeline."

Her mother's voice broke the stillness, sharp and clipped. Eva turned to see Lady Margaret standing in the doorway of the drawing room, her expression a blend of weariness and barely restrained irritation.

"I see you've taken another unannounced excursion," Margaret said, her gaze flicking briefly to Eva's disheveled hair and riding attire.

"I needed to clear my head," Eva replied evenly, stepping closer.

Margaret's eyes narrowed. "You seem to have an alarming tendency to seek solace outside these walls. Perhaps it's time you turned your attention inward—to your family and your future."

Eva straightened, her jaw tightening. "If by my future you mean Lord Fairmont, I've already made my feelings clear."

"Your feelings," Margaret repeated, her voice low and bitter. "How fortunate for you to have the luxury of considering your feelings while this estate crumbles beneath our feet."

Eva flinched, but she held her ground. "There are other ways to save Ashcombe, Mother. You refuse to see them because they don't align with your plans."

Margaret's lips pressed into a thin line, her voice trembling with barely restrained anger. "And what are these other ways, Evangeline? Enlighten me. Should we sell off more land? Beg the tenants to pay higher rents they cannot afford? Or perhaps you think Captain Grey can save us with his noble ideals?"

The mention of Nathaniel sent a jolt through Eva, but she refused to let it show. "Nathaniel has done more for this estate than Fairmont ever could. He works tirelessly to find solutions, not for himself, but for all of us."

Margaret's eyes flashed, her composure slipping. "Do not speak to me of solutions, child. You know nothing of what it takes to hold a family together, to secure a legacy."

"I know enough to see that you've sacrificed everything to preserve something that no longer exists," Eva said, her voice rising. "And now you expect me to do the same."

The silence that followed was deafening, the air between them crackling with tension. Margaret's face was pale, her eyes burning with unshed tears.

"If you walk away from this family, Evangeline," Margaret said finally, her voice breaking, "you will regret it. You will regret it every day for the rest of your life."

Eva's chest ached, her mother's words cutting deeper than she wanted to admit. But beneath the pain was a flicker of defiance, a quiet strength that had been growing steadily within her.

"I'm not walking away," Eva said softly, her voice trembling. "I'm choosing a different path."

Margaret said nothing, her silence colder than any words she could have spoken.

That evening, Eva retreated to the garden, the cool night air wrapping around her like a balm. The roses swayed gently in the breeze, their petals catching the faint glow of the moonlight.

She walked the familiar paths, her steps slow and deliberate as she tried to quiet the storm raging inside her. Her mother's words echoed in her mind, their weight pressing down on her chest.

She didn't hear Nathaniel approach until he was standing beside her, his presence steady and grounding.

"I thought I'd find you here," he said, his voice low.

Eva glanced at him, her lips curving into a faint smile. "Do you make a habit of watching over me, Captain Grey?"

"Only when it seems necessary," he replied, his tone light but his gaze serious.

They stood in silence for a moment, the hum of the night settling around them. Eva stared at the roses, her thoughts a tangle of emotions she couldn't untangle.

"My mother thinks I'm abandoning the family," she said finally, her voice barely above a whisper.

Nathaniel frowned, his jaw tightening. "You're not abandoning them, Eva. You're trying to save them in a way she doesn't understand."

"But what if she's right?" Eva asked, turning to face him. "What if I'm being selfish?"

"You're not selfish," Nathaniel said firmly. "You're brave enough to fight for what you believe in, even when it's hard. That's not selfish—it's necessary."

His words sent a wave of emotion crashing over her, and she felt her resolve waver. "I don't know if I can keep doing this," she said, her voice breaking.

Nathaniel stepped closer, his gaze steady and unwavering. "You can, Eva. And you will. Because you care too much to let this place, these people, fall apart."

Her breath caught, his words piercing through the doubts that clung to her. She looked up at him, her heart pounding in her chest.

"You believe in me more than I believe in myself," she said softly.

Nathaniel's expression softened, and he reached out, his hand brushing lightly against hers. "Because I see who you are, Eva. And I know what you're capable of."

The warmth of his touch sent a shiver through her, and for a moment, the weight of the world seemed to lift. She met his gaze, her chest tightening with a mix of fear and longing.

"Nathaniel," she began, her voice trembling, "I—"

The sound of footsteps on the gravel path interrupted her, and they both turned to see Sophia approaching, her expression anxious.

"Eva," Sophia called, her voice cutting through the quiet. "Mother is asking for you."

Eva swallowed hard, her gaze lingering on Nathaniel for a moment longer. "I'll be there in a moment."

Sophia hesitated, then nodded, disappearing back toward the house.

Eva turned back to Nathaniel, her heart aching with the words she hadn't been able to say. "Thank you," she whispered, her voice trembling.

Nathaniel nodded, his gaze soft. "Always."

As she walked back toward the manor, the moonlight casting her shadow long across the path, Eva felt the stirrings of a choice she knew she could no longer avoid.

Chapter Thirteen

The manor was quiet when Eva returned inside, the air heavy with the kind of stillness that felt more oppressive than calming. She climbed the stairs to her mother's sitting room, her footsteps muffled against the runner that lined the wooden staircase. Her heart pounded in her chest, each beat echoing louder than the last.

When she reached the door, she hesitated for a moment before knocking lightly.

"Come in," Lady Margaret's voice called, cool and controlled.

Eva pushed the door open to find her mother seated at her desk, a pile of correspondence spread before her. Margaret didn't look up immediately, her pen gliding smoothly across the paper in front of her.

"You asked for me?" Eva said, stepping into the room.

Margaret set the pen down, folding her hands neatly atop the desk as she finally met Eva's gaze. "Yes. Sit."

Eva obeyed, sinking into the chair opposite her mother. The silence that followed was deliberate, calculated, as Margaret allowed the tension to settle over them.

"I've given your behavior considerable thought," Margaret began, her tone measured. "And I've decided to extend you a final opportunity to correct your course."

Eva stiffened, her jaw tightening. "And what does that entail?"

"You will accept Lord Fairmont's proposal," Margaret said simply. "And you will do so without further delay."

"No," Eva said, the word slipping out before she could temper it.

Margaret's eyes narrowed, her hands tightening slightly atop the desk. "You will not refuse me, Evangeline. This is not a matter of preference—it is a necessity."

"It is not a necessity," Eva said firmly. "It is your obsession with control, your refusal to consider that there might be another way to save Ashcombe."

Margaret stood abruptly, the legs of her chair scraping against the floor. "Do not presume to understand what is at stake here. You are young, idealistic, and blind to the realities of this world. Fairmont offers stability, security—"

"Fairmont offers servitude," Eva interrupted, rising to her feet. "He doesn't want me, Mother. He wants the estate, the title. He sees me as a transaction, a means to an end."

Margaret's face flushed with anger. "And what of Captain Grey? Do you think he can save you with his noble speeches and his farmer's hands? Do you imagine that the villagers will flock to your side if you turn your back on the very society that sustains us?"

Eva flinched at the venom in her mother's words, but she didn't falter. "Nathaniel may not be a lord, but he has more honor and compassion than Fairmont could ever hope to possess. He doesn't see people as tools, Mother. He sees them as human beings."

The silence that followed was deafening, the tension between them crackling like a storm about to break.

Margaret exhaled sharply, her expression hardening. "You are a fool, Evangeline. A foolish, stubborn girl who doesn't understand the consequences of her actions."

"And you are a woman so consumed by fear that you've forgotten what it means to live," Eva said softly, her voice trembling with emotion.

Margaret's lips parted, her breath hitching, but no words came.

"I will not marry Fairmont," Eva said firmly. "And if you cannot accept that, then I will leave Ashcombe. But I will not sacrifice my freedom to preserve an illusion of security."

She turned and left the room before her mother could respond, her heart pounding in her chest as she made her way down the hall.

Eva found herself back in the garden, the cool night air wrapping around her like a balm. She wandered the familiar paths, her steps unsteady as the weight of the confrontation with her mother settled over her.

She paused by the trellis, her hand brushing lightly against the roses. Their petals were soft beneath her fingers, their scent heady and bittersweet.

"You're not running this time."

The sound of Nathaniel's voice made her turn, her breath catching as she saw him standing a few paces away.

"Not this time," she said softly, a faint smile tugging at her lips.

Nathaniel stepped closer, his gaze steady and unwavering. "How did it go?"

"As expected," Eva replied, her voice tinged with weariness. "My mother and I rarely see eye to eye these days."

Nathaniel nodded, his jaw tightening. "You're stronger than she gives you credit for."

Eva looked away, her chest tightening. "I don't feel strong."

"You are," he said firmly. "And you're not alone."

His words sent a rush of warmth through her, and she turned back to him, her heart pounding. "Nathaniel... why do you care so much?"

His gaze softened, his expression unguarded for the first time. "Because you make me believe in something again. In hope. In resilience. In everything I thought I'd lost."

The raw honesty in his voice left her breathless, and she took a step closer, her hand brushing against his.

"Nathaniel," she whispered, her voice trembling.

He reached up, his fingers lightly tracing the curve of her cheek. "Eva."

The world seemed to still around them, the hum of the night fading into silence. For a moment, everything else disappeared—the weight of the estate, the expectations of society, the walls they had both built around themselves.

And then he leaned in, his lips brushing against hers with a tenderness that made her heart ache. The kiss was soft, hesitant, but filled with a quiet intensity that left her breathless.

When they parted, Nathaniel rested his forehead against hers, his breath warm against her skin.

"I'm with you," he said softly. "Whatever you decide, I'm with you."

Tears pricked at Eva's eyes, and she nodded, her voice breaking as she whispered, "Thank you."

As they stood together in the moonlit garden, Eva felt something shift within her—a quiet strength she hadn't realized she possessed. For the first time, she felt ready to face whatever came next.

Chapter Fourteen

The dawn light filtered through Eva's window, soft and golden, casting long shadows across the floor. She sat at her writing desk, staring down at a blank sheet of paper, the quill in her hand hovering just above the page. Her heart still raced from the night before, Nathaniel's words and touch lingering like an imprint on her soul.

She hadn't slept, her mind too restless with questions and possibilities. For so long, her life had felt like a series of choices made for her, a path laid out by her mother and the weight of Ashcombe's legacy. But now, for the first time, she felt as though she was standing at a crossroads of her own making.

The soft knock at her door broke her reverie.

"Come in," she called, setting the quill down.

Sophia entered, her curls slightly mussed and her expression curious. She carried a plate of toast and a cup of tea, setting them down on the desk with a flourish.

"You missed breakfast," Sophia said, perching on the edge of the bed.

"I wasn't hungry," Eva replied, though her stomach grumbled faintly in protest.

Sophia tilted her head, studying her sister with a knowing smile. "You look different this morning. Lighter, maybe."

Eva raised an eyebrow, her lips twitching into a faint smile. "Is that so?"

Sophia nodded, her grin widening. "Did something happen last night? You've been positively dreary for days, and now you seem... hopeful."

Eva hesitated, her cheeks warming as memories of the garden flooded her mind. "I... spoke with Nathaniel."

Sophia's eyes lit up, and she leaned forward eagerly. "And?"

"And," Eva said, her voice soft, "he reminded me that I'm not alone."

Sophia's expression softened, her grin fading into something gentler. "You've always had me, you know. And now him too, it seems."

Eva reached out, taking her sister's hand. "I know. And I'm grateful for both of you."

Sophia squeezed her hand, her blue eyes shining with affection. "So, what will you do now?"

Eva glanced at the blank page on her desk, her resolve hardening. "I'll fight. For Ashcombe, for myself, and for the people who deserve better than what we've given them."

Sophia smiled, her pride evident. "You'll be brilliant, Eva."

Later that morning, Eva made her way to the study where Nathaniel was pouring over estate ledgers, his sleeves rolled up and his brow furrowed in concentration. He looked up as she entered, his expression softening.

"Lady Ashcombe," he said, rising from his chair.

"Nathaniel," she replied, her voice steady but warm. "I need your help."

He gestured for her to sit, and she took the chair across from him, her hands folded neatly in her lap.

"I want to explore alternative solutions for the estate," Eva said, her tone firm. "Fairmont's proposal is not the answer, but we cannot ignore the financial reality we're facing. There must be another way."

Nathaniel leaned forward, his expression thoughtful. "There are ways to modernize without surrendering control to someone like

Fairmont. Crop rotation, new farming techniques, careful investment in infrastructure. It won't be easy, but it's possible."

Eva nodded, determination sparking in her eyes. "Then let's begin. Show me the numbers, the options. I want to understand every aspect of this estate, not just as a mistress, but as a steward."

Nathaniel smiled faintly, admiration shining in his gaze. "You're serious about this."

"I am," Eva said firmly. "And I won't let anyone—Fairmont, my mother, or anyone else—stand in the way of what's right for Ashcombe."

For the next few hours, they worked side by side, pouring over maps, accounts, and tenant records. Nathaniel explained the intricacies of crop yields and land management with patience, his passion for the land evident in every word.

Eva listened intently, asking questions and offering ideas where she could. She felt a strange exhilaration in the work, a sense of purpose she hadn't felt in years.

By the time the sun reached its zenith, they had sketched out the beginnings of a plan—a detailed strategy for revitalizing the estate without sacrificing its soul.

"This is just the start," Nathaniel said, leaning back in his chair. "There's much more to consider, and the villagers will need to be involved. But it's a foundation."

Eva smiled, a sense of pride swelling in her chest. "It's more than I could have hoped for. Thank you, Nathaniel."

He shook his head, his gaze steady. "You're the one who's doing this, Eva. I'm just here to help."

Her heart fluttered at the sincerity in his voice, and she reached out, her hand brushing lightly against his. "I couldn't do it without you."

Nathaniel hesitated, his gaze searching hers. "And I wouldn't want you to."

The moment stretched between them, the weight of unspoken feelings lingering in the air. But before either could speak, a knock at the door broke the spell.

"Lady Ashcombe," the butler called, his voice muffled. "Your mother requests your presence in the drawing room."

Eva sighed, her resolve hardening once more. "It seems my work is never done."

Nathaniel smiled faintly, his hand retreating from hers. "Go. I'll be here when you're ready."

As she stood and left the study, Eva felt a quiet strength building within her. The path ahead would be difficult, but for the first time, she felt as though she wasn't walking it alone.

Chapter Fifteen

The drawing room was filled with an uncomfortable tension as Eva entered. Lady Margaret stood by the window, her back rigid, the drapery clasped in one hand as she stared out at the garden. Her usual poise seemed more forced than ever, her silence a heavier rebuke than words might have been.

"Mother," Eva said softly, stepping into the room.

Margaret turned, her lips pressed into a thin line. "You've kept me waiting."

"I was working with Nathaniel on the estate's accounts," Eva replied evenly.

Margaret's eyes narrowed, her disapproval sharp. "The estate's accounts. And what wisdom has Captain Grey imparted upon you? Has he filled your head with more of his rustic idealism?"

Eva drew a steadying breath, her posture straightening. "He's shown me that there are alternatives to Fairmont's offer—ones that don't involve selling Ashcombe's soul."

Margaret released the drapery, her movements sharp as she crossed the room. "You speak as though this estate is nothing more than bricks and mortar, Evangeline. Ashcombe is legacy, history. It requires sacrifices you seem unwilling to make."

Eva clenched her hands into fists at her sides. "I am willing to make sacrifices, Mother, but not my autonomy. And certainly not for a man like Fairmont."

Margaret's expression faltered, a flicker of vulnerability crossing her face before she masked it with anger. "You think I enjoy pushing you toward this marriage? You think I do it for myself?"

"I think you've forgotten that Ashcombe is not the only thing that matters," Eva said, her voice trembling with emotion. "There is more to life than survival. There's love, happiness, purpose—and you've spent so long preserving the past that you've lost sight of the future."

Margaret's shoulders stiffened, but she said nothing, her silence more telling than any argument.

"I will save this estate," Eva continued, her tone soft but resolute. "But I will do it my way."

For a long moment, Margaret didn't respond. Then, with a tight nod, she turned back to the window. "Do what you will, Evangeline. But don't come crying to me when you fail."

Eva felt the sting of her mother's words, but she held her ground. Without another word, she left the room, the weight of the confrontation pressing heavily on her chest.

Outside, the crisp autumn air was a welcome relief. Eva wandered the garden paths, her footsteps unhurried as she let the tension drain from her body. The roses swayed gently in the breeze, their petals still vibrant despite the changing season.

She didn't have to look far to find Nathaniel. He was near the stables, speaking with one of the grooms. His sleeves were rolled up, his hands dusted with dirt, and the sight of him—steady, grounded—filled Eva with a quiet sense of calm.

Nathaniel glanced up as she approached, his expression softening. "How did it go?"

"About as well as expected," Eva replied, her lips curving into a faint smile.

Nathaniel dismissed the groom with a nod, then turned his full attention to her. "Your mother is... difficult to persuade, I take it."

"That's an understatement," Eva said with a wry laugh. "But I think she's finally beginning to see that I won't back down."

Nathaniel smiled, a flicker of pride in his eyes. "Good. You shouldn't."

They fell into step together, walking along the edge of the garden where the roses gave way to wild grasses and the rolling hills beyond.

"There's something else I wanted to tell you," Eva said after a moment, her voice quieter now.

Nathaniel glanced at her, his brow furrowing slightly. "What is it?"

"I've been thinking," Eva began, choosing her words carefully, "about what it would mean to truly move forward. To embrace the future, not just for Ashcombe, but for myself."

Nathaniel's steps slowed, his gaze steady. "And what have you decided?"

Eva stopped, turning to face him fully. "That I don't want to face it alone. That I want to fight for this place, for these people—but also for the things that make life worth living."

Nathaniel's eyes softened, his expression unguarded. "Eva..."

"I know it won't be easy," she said, her voice trembling. "But I've spent so long trying to be everything my mother wanted, everything society expects. And now, I just want to be myself."

Nathaniel reached out, his hand brushing lightly against hers. "You're not alone, Eva. You never have been."

Her breath caught, the warmth of his touch grounding her. "I don't know what the future holds," she said softly. "But I know I want you to be a part of it."

Nathaniel's gaze searched hers, and then, without hesitation, he pulled her into a gentle embrace. "I'll be with you," he murmured, his voice steady and sure. "For as long as you'll have me."

Eva closed her eyes, her head resting against his chest as the steady rhythm of his heartbeat echoed in her ears. For the first time, she felt a sense of peace, a quiet certainty that the path she had chosen—difficult as it might be—was the right one.

Nathaniel and Eva lingered near the edge of the garden, the quiet between them not awkward but charged with meaning. The world around them seemed to settle into stillness, the only sounds the faint rustling of leaves and the distant chirp of crickets.

"You're certain about this?" Nathaniel asked finally, his voice low but steady.

Eva tilted her head, her gaze tracing the far hills where the horizon met the sky. "About choosing this path? Yes. About how to navigate it? Not yet."

Nathaniel's lips curved into a faint smile, and he leaned against the garden's low stone wall, his arms crossing over his chest. "That's the nature of change—it rarely comes with a map."

She looked at him, her own smile tugging at the corners of her lips. "Is that wisdom from your military days?"

His gaze softened, and a faraway look crossed his face. "Partly. War teaches you many things, Eva. Most of all, it teaches you that certainty is a luxury."

Her smile faded slightly at the weight of his words. "Do you miss it?"

Nathaniel hesitated, his expression clouding for a moment before he answered. "I miss the purpose it gave me. The clarity. But I don't miss what it asked of me—the choices, the sacrifices."

Eva nodded, her chest tightening at the thought of what he must have endured. "And now?"

He met her gaze, his expression unflinching. "Now, I'm here. And I find purpose in the land, the people, and... in helping you."

Her breath caught, the sincerity in his voice cutting through her like a blade. "Nathaniel," she began, but the words caught in her throat.

He straightened, stepping closer to her, his gaze searching hers. "You don't have to say anything. I just... I need you to know that whatever happens, you don't have to face it alone."

The quiet strength in his words sent a shiver through her, and for a moment, she let herself lean into the warmth of his presence, the steady anchor he had become in her life.

"Thank you," she said softly, her voice trembling. "You've been a better friend to me than I ever could have asked for."

Nathaniel's jaw tightened, and he glanced away briefly, as though composing himself. "It's more than friendship, Eva."

Her heart skipped a beat, and she turned fully to him, her hands curling at her sides. "I know," she said, her voice barely above a whisper.

For a moment, the air between them was electric, the tension building as unspoken feelings hovered just beyond reach. Then Nathaniel stepped back, his expression unreadable.

"We should head back," he said quietly.

Eva nodded, the moment slipping away as quickly as it had come.

When they returned to the manor, the quiet bustle of the household was a stark contrast to the stillness of the garden. Eva parted ways with Nathaniel, each offering the other a faint smile before disappearing into separate corridors.

As Eva walked toward her rooms, Sophia appeared at her side, her curls bouncing as she fell into step.

"You've been with Captain Grey again," Sophia teased, her tone light but probing.

Eva rolled her eyes, though her cheeks flushed. "We were discussing estate matters."

Sophia grinned. "Is that what they're calling it now?"

"Sophia," Eva warned, though a faint smile tugged at her lips.

Her sister's grin faded slightly, and she touched Eva's arm, her voice softening. "You seem... different. Happier, maybe."

Eva paused, her chest tightening. "Do I?"

Sophia nodded, her expression earnest. "I'm glad, Eva. You deserve it. Whatever it is that's making you feel this way, hold onto it."

Eva blinked back a sudden rush of emotion, pulling Sophia into a quick hug. "Thank you, Sophia. For everything."

Sophia hugged her back tightly before stepping away, her smile brighter than ever. "Now, go write your letters or plot your rebellion or whatever it is you do in that room of yours. I'll see you at supper."

Eva laughed softly as Sophia darted off, her heart feeling lighter than it had in weeks.

The rest of the day passed in quiet preparation. Eva spent the afternoon reviewing Nathaniel's notes on the estate and drafting letters to several nearby landowners who had expressed interest in collaborative farming practices. Her resolve grew with each line she wrote, the plan beginning to take shape in her mind.

By evening, as the household gathered for supper, Eva felt a new sense of purpose guiding her steps.

The dining room was lively, with Sophia animatedly recounting some tale of mischief she'd witnessed in the village, her laughter infectious even to their father, who often drifted into absentminded musings. Lady Margaret remained reserved, her cool demeanor a stark contrast to the warmth of the room.

But Eva wasn't deterred. She addressed her mother with calm confidence.

"Mother," Eva said, setting her fork down and meeting Margaret's gaze. "I've made progress on a plan for Ashcombe."

Margaret arched an eyebrow, her expression skeptical. "Have you, now?"

"Yes," Eva replied evenly. "I've been working with Captain Grey on strategies for modernizing the estate—crop rotation, reinvestment in infrastructure, and fostering partnerships with nearby landowners. It will require effort and cooperation, but it's a viable path forward."

"And what does Lord Fairmont think of this plan?" Margaret asked, her tone sharp.

Eva's spine stiffened. "I have not consulted him. Nor do I intend to. This is my decision, and it's one I believe is best for Ashcombe."

The room fell silent, all eyes on Lady Margaret as she regarded Eva with a mixture of disbelief and reluctant respect.

"Bold words," Margaret said finally, her voice quieter but no less commanding. "We shall see if you can back them with action."

"I intend to," Eva said, her voice firm.

Sophia beamed across the table, and even their father nodded faintly, as though acknowledging Eva's growing resolve.

As the meal continued, Eva felt a spark of hope ignite within her. The road ahead would be difficult, but she was no longer afraid to walk it.

And as Nathaniel's steady gaze met hers across the room, she knew she wouldn't be walking it alone.

Chapter Sixteen

The following morning dawned crisp and clear, the first golden rays of sunlight casting long shadows across the Ashcombe estate. Eva stood at the edge of the garden, the morning chill nipping at her skin. She had risen before the household, unable to stay in bed as her thoughts churned.

Today would mark a turning point. For months, she had allowed herself to be swept along by the tide of expectations and obligations. Now, she would plant her feet firmly, ready to face what lay ahead.

Her plan with Nathaniel had taken shape into something tangible, something actionable. The letters she had written to the nearby landowners had been sent with a messenger before dawn, her words carefully chosen to appeal to their sense of community and shared prosperity.

The estate's steward had been surprised by her decisiveness when she'd asked for an updated ledger of accounts. The villagers, she hoped, would come to see her as someone willing to fight for their livelihoods rather than sell them out to Fairmont's ambitions.

But one challenge still loomed, one she had yet to fully confront: her mother's simmering resistance and Fairmont's growing impatience.

As the morning wore on, Eva found herself seated at the breakfast table with Sophia and their father. Margaret's absence was conspicuous, though not entirely unexpected.

"I think Mother is hiding," Sophia said with a grin, buttering a slice of bread.

"She's probably just... regrouping," Eva replied, though her tone lacked conviction.

"From you?" Sophia asked with mock incredulity. "The mighty Lady Ashcombe bested by her own daughter?"

Eva couldn't help but laugh softly, though the sound was tinged with nervousness. "Hardly. I'm sure she's planning her next move."

Their father glanced up from his tea, his pale blue eyes flickering with a rare moment of lucidity. "Your mother's heart is in the right place, Evangeline," he said, his voice soft but clear. "She loves this family. She just... expresses it poorly."

Eva nodded, her chest tightening. "I know, Father."

Sophia's lighthearted expression softened, and for a moment, the sisters exchanged a glance of mutual understanding.

Later that morning, Eva made her way to the stables. She had promised Nathaniel they would inspect the eastern fields together, and the prospect of spending time with him, away from the tensions of the house, was a welcome reprieve.

He was waiting for her when she arrived, his shirt sleeves rolled up and his hands dusted with hay. He turned as she approached, his smile faint but warm.

"Ready to ride?" he asked, gesturing toward the two saddled horses.

Eva nodded, her heart lifting at the sight of him. "More than ready."

They rode in comfortable silence, the rhythmic sound of the horses' hooves blending with the rustle of the wind through the trees. The path took them along the edges of the estate, where the land opened up into vast fields dotted with patches of wildflowers.

When they reached the eastern boundary, Nathaniel dismounted, helping Eva down before tying the horses to a nearby tree.

"This area has the most potential," he said, gesturing to the gently sloping fields before them. "The soil is fertile, and with proper crop rotation, it could yield enough to support both the estate and the village."

Eva stepped closer, her gaze sweeping over the land. "It's beautiful," she said softly.

Nathaniel nodded, his expression thoughtful. "It's more than that—it's life. For the people here, for the estate. But it'll take hard work and trust to make it happen."

Eva turned to him, her chest tightening. "You speak as if you're asking something of me."

"I am," Nathaniel said, his gaze steady. "I'm asking you to trust yourself. To trust that what you're doing is right, even if it's difficult."

She looked away, her emotions threatening to overwhelm her. "It's easier to trust you than it is to trust myself."

Nathaniel stepped closer, his voice soft but firm. "Then let me help you. Let me be the one you lean on when it feels like too much."

Eva's breath hitched, her heart pounding as his words sank in. She met his gaze, the weight of his sincerity pulling her in.

"Nathaniel," she began, her voice trembling, "you've already done so much for me. For Ashcombe. I don't know if I could ask for more."

"You don't have to ask," he said, his hand brushing lightly against hers. "I'm here because I want to be. Because I believe in you."

Her chest tightened, tears prickling at the corners of her eyes. "I don't deserve you."

"You deserve more than you know," he said softly.

For a moment, the world seemed to fade away, leaving only the two of them standing amidst the fields, the sunlight casting a warm glow over the land.

Before Eva could respond, the distant sound of hoofbeats broke the spell. They turned to see a rider approaching, his coat unmistakable even from afar.

"Fairmont," Nathaniel muttered, his jaw tightening.

Eva's stomach sank, but she squared her shoulders, her resolve hardening. "Let him come."

Fairmont reined in his horse a few yards away, dismounting with practiced ease. His smile was tight, his gaze flicking between Eva and Nathaniel with barely concealed disdain.

"Lady Ashcombe," he said, bowing slightly. "Captain Grey."

"Lord Fairmont," Eva replied, her tone cool.

"I couldn't help but notice you weren't at the manor," Fairmont said, his voice oozing charm. "Imagine my surprise to find you here, inspecting the fields with... your steward."

Eva lifted her chin, refusing to rise to his bait. "The land is the heart of Ashcombe, my lord. It's only natural that I would take an interest in its care."

Fairmont's smile tightened further, his gaze darkening. "A noble sentiment. But one wonders if such work is best left to those better suited to it."

Nathaniel stiffened, but Eva placed a calming hand on his arm before stepping forward. "I trust Captain Grey's expertise implicitly," she said, her voice firm. "He has been invaluable to Ashcombe, and to me."

Fairmont's eyes narrowed, his mask of civility slipping. "You put a great deal of faith in him, my lady. I hope it does not lead to... complications."

Eva's pulse quickened, but she held her ground. "The only complications I foresee, Lord Fairmont, are those caused by men who refuse to adapt to a changing world."

Fairmont's jaw tightened, but he offered a stiff bow. "I see I have interrupted your work. I shall take my leave."

As he mounted his horse and rode away, Nathaniel turned to Eva, his expression a mixture of admiration and concern.

"You handled that well," he said.

Eva exhaled, the tension draining from her shoulders. "I couldn't have done it without you."

Nathaniel's lips curved into a faint smile. "You're stronger than you think, Eva."

She looked at him, her heart swelling with gratitude and something deeper, something she wasn't ready to name.

"Let's get back to work," she said, her voice steady.

Nathaniel nodded, and together, they turned back to the land, ready to face whatever challenges lay ahead.

Chapter Seventeen

By late afternoon, the tension of Fairmont's visit had dissipated, replaced by a renewed focus on the work at hand. Eva and Nathaniel had spent hours walking the eastern fields, discussing crop plans, fencing repairs, and irrigation systems. The clarity and purpose of their shared vision energized Eva, and for the first time in months, she felt like she was shaping her destiny rather than being swept along by it.

As they rode back toward the manor, the horses' steady pace matched the comforting rhythm of Eva's thoughts. Nathaniel rode beside her, his presence a constant, grounding force.

"You've made real progress today," he said, breaking the companionable silence.

"We've made progress," Eva corrected, casting him a grateful smile.

Nathaniel tilted his head, his lips twitching into a faint smile. "Fair enough."

As they approached the stables, the sprawling estate came into view, bathed in the golden light of the setting sun. The manor's weathered stone facade gleamed warmly, the roses in the garden casting long, soft shadows across the lawn.

Eva dismounted first, handing the reins to a waiting stable hand. She turned to Nathaniel as he swung down from his saddle with practiced ease.

"You've given me hope," she said softly, her gaze steady.

Nathaniel paused, his expression softening. "It was always there, Eva. You just needed a reason to believe in it."

Her chest tightened at the warmth in his words, but before she could respond, a voice called from the manor steps.

"Lady Ashcombe!"

They both turned to see Sophia rushing toward them, her curls bouncing as she waved a folded piece of paper in the air.

"What is it?" Eva asked, stepping forward.

"It's a letter," Sophia said breathlessly, holding it out. "From one of the landowners you wrote to."

Eva took the letter, her hands trembling slightly as she unfolded it. Nathaniel stepped closer, his gaze scanning her face as she read.

"Well?" Sophia asked, practically vibrating with anticipation.

Eva looked up, her eyes shining. "It's from Lord Whitlock. He's interested in the plan and wants to meet to discuss it further."

Sophia clapped her hands together, beaming. "That's wonderful!"

Nathaniel's smile was subtle but no less genuine. "It's a start," he said.

Eva nodded, her heart swelling with a mix of relief and excitement. "It's more than that—it's an opportunity."

The evening meal was a quieter affair, with Sophia's enthusiasm the only bright spot against Margaret's cold silence. Their father seemed preoccupied, his usual absentminded musings keeping him distant from the conversation.

Eva ate sparingly, her mind focused on the letter from Lord Whitlock and the possibilities it represented. She could feel her mother's disapproval radiating across the table, but she refused to let it deter her.

As the meal concluded, Eva excused herself, retreating to the library where Nathaniel was waiting.

He stood near the fire, his sleeves rolled up and a ledger in his hands. He looked up as she entered, his expression shifting to one of quiet anticipation.

"How was dinner?" he asked, setting the ledger aside.

"As tense as expected," Eva replied with a faint smile. "But Sophia was delighted by the letter from Lord Whitlock."

"And you?" Nathaniel asked, stepping closer.

Eva met his gaze, her smile softening. "I'm... hopeful. It feels like the first real step toward something better."

Nathaniel nodded, his hazel eyes steady. "It's a good step. And it's yours."

She looked away, her fingers brushing absently against the locket around her neck. "I couldn't have done it without you, Nathaniel."

"You give me too much credit," he said, his tone quiet.

"And you give yourself too little," she replied, her gaze returning to his.

The air between them grew heavy, the unspoken feelings they had danced around for weeks now impossible to ignore. Eva took a slow breath, her chest tightening as she stepped closer.

"Nathaniel," she began, her voice trembling slightly, "I don't know where this path will lead, but I do know one thing."

"What's that?" he asked, his voice low and steady.

"I want you to be part of it," she said, her words barely above a whisper.

His expression softened, a flicker of vulnerability crossing his face. "Eva... you don't know how much that means to me."

She reached out, her fingers brushing lightly against his. "Then stay. Stay and fight with me."

Nathaniel's hand closed around hers, his grip firm but gentle. "Always," he said softly.

For a moment, the world seemed to fall away, leaving only the warmth of his presence and the steady rhythm of their breathing.

Then, as if sensing the gravity of the moment, Nathaniel released her hand and stepped back slightly. "There's still much to do," he said, his tone practical but kind.

Eva smiled faintly, nodding. "Then we should get to it."

The night stretched on as they worked side by side, mapping out strategies and refining their plans. The flickering firelight cast warm shadows across the room, the quiet hum of their voices blending with the crackle of the flames.

As the hours slipped by, Eva felt a sense of calm settle over her—a quiet certainty that, for the first time in a long while, she was exactly where she needed to be.

Chapter Eighteen

The morning was alive with quiet determination. The arrival of Lord Whitlock's letter had invigorated the household, though only Sophia openly celebrated the news. Lady Margaret remained aloof, her silence more pointed than any words she might have spoken.

Eva, however, refused to let her mother's icy demeanor dampen her resolve. The wheels had been set in motion, and she was determined to see the plan through.

Nathaniel was already in the stables when Eva arrived, his shirt sleeves rolled up as he secured the saddle on his horse. The rhythmic sound of leather and buckles was a comforting prelude to the day's task: meeting Lord Whitlock to discuss their shared vision for Ashcombe's future.

"Good morning," Eva said as she approached.

Nathaniel glanced up, a faint smile tugging at the corners of his lips. "Good morning, my lady. Ready for your first diplomatic mission?"

She laughed softly, shaking her head. "Let's hope I'm as persuasive on the ride as I was in my letter."

"I have no doubt," he said, his voice steady. "Whitlock wouldn't have responded if he weren't already intrigued. The rest is about showing him you mean what you say."

Eva nodded, her chest tightening with both nerves and excitement. "Then let's not keep him waiting."

The ride to Whitlock Manor took them through rolling hills and wooded paths, the scenery shifting from the familiar fields of

Ashcombe to the more manicured lands of their neighbor. Whitlock Manor was smaller than Ashcombe, but its elegance was undeniable. The neatly trimmed hedges and ivy-covered walls spoke of quiet prosperity, a stark contrast to the fraying edges of her own estate.

Lord Whitlock greeted them in the garden, a tall man in his early forties with salt-and-pepper hair and an air of affable curiosity. He extended his hand to Eva as they dismounted, his smile warm but assessing.

"Lady Ashcombe," he said. "It's a pleasure to finally meet you."

"Lord Whitlock," Eva replied, shaking his hand. "Thank you for agreeing to meet with us."

"And you must be Captain Grey," Whitlock said, turning to Nathaniel. "I've heard of your work on the estate. Impressive, by all accounts."

"Thank you, my lord," Nathaniel replied, his tone respectful but reserved.

Whitlock gestured toward a shaded table set with tea and light refreshments. "Shall we?"

The meeting began with polite pleasantries, Whitlock inquiring after Ashcombe's history and current state with genuine interest. Eva answered each question with careful honesty, her words painting a vivid picture of the estate's struggles and her vision for its revival.

"I must admit," Whitlock said, setting down his teacup, "I was surprised by your letter, Lady Ashcombe. Many in your position might have chosen an easier path—aligning with a more influential partner, for instance."

Eva's cheeks flushed, but she held his gaze. "I believe in Ashcombe's independence, my lord. I'm not looking for someone to take it over. I'm looking for a partnership—one built on mutual respect and shared prosperity."

Whitlock nodded thoughtfully, his expression softening. "A noble stance. And not an easy one."

"Few things worth doing are," Eva said, a faint smile tugging at her lips.

Whitlock turned his attention to Nathaniel. "And what role do you see yourself playing in this, Captain?"

Nathaniel straightened, his voice steady and confident. "My role is to support Lady Ashcombe's vision, my lord. I believe in what she's trying to achieve—not just for the estate, but for the community it sustains."

Whitlock studied them both for a moment, his expression unreadable. Then he leaned back in his chair, a small smile breaking through.

"I like you, Lady Ashcombe," he said. "And I respect your courage in seeking me out. I'll admit, I've been considering modernizing my own estate's practices, but I hadn't found the right catalyst. Perhaps this is it."

Eva's heart lifted, and she leaned forward slightly. "Does that mean you're willing to join us?"

Whitlock nodded. "It means I'm willing to explore the possibility. Let's begin with a trial partnership—shared resources, collaborative efforts on crop management, and an exchange of ideas. If it proves successful, we can formalize something more permanent."

"That's all I could ask for," Eva said, her voice filled with gratitude.

Whitlock stood, extending his hand once more. "Then let's make it happen."

Eva rose to shake his hand, the weight of his words sinking in. This was more than a step forward—it was a leap.

The ride back to Ashcombe was quieter, though the energy between Eva and Nathaniel crackled with unspoken excitement.

"We did it," Eva said finally, her voice soft but triumphant.

"You did it," Nathaniel corrected, his smile warm.

She turned to him, her eyes shining. "I couldn't have done it without you."

He shrugged, his tone teasing. "I'm just here to hold the reins."

Eva laughed, the sound light and free. "You're far more than that, Nathaniel Grey. Don't you dare diminish your role in this."

He glanced at her, his expression softening. "Fair enough."

As they approached the manor, the first lights of evening flickered to life in the windows. The sight filled Eva with a renewed sense of purpose. There was still much to do, but for the first time, she felt as though the future was something she could shape with her own hands.

Later that evening, after supper, Eva found herself back in the library. The fire crackled softly in the hearth, casting warm light across the room. She sat at her desk, a fresh sheet of paper before her as she drafted a summary of the day's progress to share with the steward and the tenants.

A knock at the door drew her attention, and Nathaniel stepped inside, his presence filling the room with quiet assurance.

"How are you feeling?" he asked, closing the door behind him.

"Tired," Eva admitted, setting down her pen. "But hopeful."

Nathaniel crossed the room, leaning against the edge of the desk. "You've earned that hope, Eva. Today was a victory."

She smiled, her chest swelling with gratitude. "Thank you, Nathaniel. For everything."

He shook his head, his gaze steady. "You don't need to thank me. I'm here because I believe in you."

Her breath caught, and for a moment, the world seemed to still. The firelight danced in his eyes, and the weight of unspoken feelings hung in the air between them.

"Nathaniel," she began, her voice trembling, "I—"

He leaned forward slightly, his voice soft. "You don't have to say anything."

But she shook her head, her hand reaching out to brush lightly against his. "Yes, I do. You've been my anchor, my guide—and more than that, my friend. I don't know what I would have done without you."

Nathaniel's hand covered hers, his touch warm and grounding. "You would have found your way, Eva. Because that's who you are."

Her heart swelled, the intensity of his gaze drawing her in. "And who am I to you?" she whispered.

Nathaniel hesitated, his expression unguarded. "You're everything."

The weight of his words left her breathless, and for a moment, all she could do was stare at him, her chest tightening with emotions she could no longer ignore.

"Nathaniel," she murmured, her voice trembling.

Before she could say more, he leaned in, his lips brushing against hers in a kiss that was soft, tentative, and filled with a quiet intensity that stole her breath.

When they parted, he rested his forehead against hers, his voice barely above a whisper. "I'm with you, Eva. Always."

Tears pricked at her eyes, and she nodded, her heart overflowing with emotions she hadn't dared to name until now. "Always," she echoed.

As the fire crackled softly behind them, Eva knew she had found not only her purpose but also her partner in the journey ahead.

Chapter Nineteen

The next morning dawned with a clarity that mirrored Eva's mood. She rose earlier than usual, the first streaks of sunlight painting her room in shades of gold and rose. The memory of the previous night lingered, warm and vivid, filling her with a sense of quiet confidence.

Nathaniel's words and the tenderness of their shared moment had settled something deep within her, solidifying her resolve to face whatever challenges lay ahead. Ashcombe's future was no longer a shadowy question—it was a path she was beginning to see clearly, one she was determined to walk with strength and purpose.

As she stepped into the dining room, she found Sophia already at the table, nibbling on a slice of toast while perusing a well-worn novel. Her sister looked up, a teasing smile spreading across her face.

"You're up early," Sophia remarked. "What's the occasion? Or should I say, who?"

Eva raised an eyebrow, though a faint blush crept into her cheeks. "Must everything be a scandal in your mind, Sophia?"

"Not everything," Sophia replied with a grin. "Just the exciting parts."

Eva rolled her eyes, though her lips twitched into a smile. "I have a meeting with the steward and some of the tenants this morning. It's time to start sharing the plan."

Sophia's expression softened, her teasing giving way to admiration. "You're really doing it, aren't you? Fighting for Ashcombe on your own terms."

"Yes," Eva said, her voice steady. "I am."

Sophia set her book down, leaning forward with a conspiratorial look. "And is Captain Grey fighting with you?"

Eva hesitated, her heart skipping a beat at the mention of Nathaniel. "He's been... indispensable. But this isn't just his fight—it's mine, too."

Sophia's smile turned knowing. "Of course it is. But I think it's nice to have someone in your corner. Someone who really sees you."

Eva didn't respond, but her sister's words settled over her like a soft blanket, warm and reassuring.

By midmorning, Eva was seated in the estate office with Nathaniel and the steward, Mr. Cartwright. The room smelled faintly of parchment and ink, its large oak desk cluttered with ledgers, maps, and loose sheets of paper detailing the estate's accounts.

Cartwright was a thin, precise man with silver-rimmed spectacles that seemed perpetually perched on the edge of his nose. He adjusted them now, peering down at the document Eva had drafted.

"This is ambitious, my lady," Cartwright said, his voice careful but intrigued. "Reorganizing tenant agreements, modernizing crop practices—these are no small undertakings."

"No, they're not," Eva replied, her tone calm but firm. "But they're necessary. We can no longer afford to cling to outdated methods. If we want Ashcombe to thrive, we must adapt."

Cartwright glanced at Nathaniel, who nodded in quiet support.

"She's right," Nathaniel said. "The changes won't be easy, but they're sustainable. And the tenants will see the benefits in time."

Cartwright frowned thoughtfully, tapping his fingers against the desk. "And Lord Fairmont? He won't be pleased to hear of this."

Eva straightened in her chair, her gaze unwavering. "Lord Fairmont's opinions are no longer my concern. This is about Ashcombe and the people who depend on it—not his ambitions."

Cartwright studied her for a moment before nodding. "Very well, my lady. I'll draft the revised agreements for the tenants. It will take some time to finalize, but we can begin introducing the changes within the month."

"Thank you, Mr. Cartwright," Eva said, relief washing over her.

As the steward excused himself to begin the task, Nathaniel leaned back in his chair, his lips curving into a faint smile.

"You handled that perfectly," he said.

Eva smiled back, a spark of pride warming her chest. "It feels good to be doing something meaningful."

Nathaniel's gaze softened, and he reached out, his hand brushing lightly against hers where it rested on the desk. "You're more than meaningful, Eva. You're extraordinary."

Her breath caught, the sincerity in his voice cutting through her like a blade. But before she could respond, a sharp knock at the door interrupted the moment.

The butler stepped in, his expression carefully neutral. "Lady Ashcombe, Lord Fairmont is here. He requests an audience with you immediately."

Eva found Fairmont in the drawing room, standing near the fireplace with an air of tightly controlled impatience. His finely tailored coat and polished boots gleamed in the light, a stark contrast to the simmering displeasure in his eyes.

"Lord Fairmont," Eva said, stepping into the room. "What brings you here unannounced?"

Fairmont turned, his smile thin and forced. "Good morning, Lady Ashcombe. I thought it prudent to discuss the... developments on your estate."

Eva arched an eyebrow, her tone cool. "I wasn't aware you were keeping such close watch."

"Come now," Fairmont said, his voice smooth but edged with condescension. "We both know that Ashcombe's affairs are of great interest to me. And I couldn't help but hear rumors of a new arrangement with Lord Whitlock."

Eva's pulse quickened, but she held her ground. "Ashcombe's arrangements are no longer any concern of yours, my lord. As I've made clear before."

Fairmont's expression darkened, his charm slipping to reveal something colder. "You're playing a dangerous game, Lady Ashcombe. Aligning yourself with Whitlock, relying on Captain Grey—these choices will have consequences."

Eva's jaw tightened, her chest burning with indignation. "The only danger here, Lord Fairmont, is allowing someone like you to dictate Ashcombe's future. That is a mistake I will not make."

Fairmont stepped closer, his voice dropping to a menacing whisper. "Do you think your tenants will remain loyal when they realize how tenuous your position is? Or that Whitlock will stick by you when things grow difficult? You're clinging to a fantasy, Evangeline."

Eva met his gaze unflinchingly, her voice steady. "And you're clinging to a control you'll never have. Leave, Lord Fairmont. You're no longer welcome here."

For a moment, Fairmont's composure wavered, his frustration evident. But then he straightened, smoothing his coat with an air of forced civility.

"As you wish," he said, his tone icy. "But don't say I didn't warn you."

He strode past her and out of the room, the click of his boots against the floor echoing like a final threat.

Eva exhaled slowly, her hands trembling slightly as the weight of the confrontation settled over her. She turned to find Nathaniel standing in the doorway, his expression unreadable but his presence a quiet reassurance.

"Are you all right?" he asked softly.

Eva nodded, though her voice trembled when she spoke. "I'm fine. He's gone."

Nathaniel stepped closer, his gaze steady and filled with quiet resolve. "You stood your ground, Eva. And you were brilliant."

Her lips curved into a faint smile, and she let out a shaky laugh. "I didn't feel brilliant."

"You are," Nathaniel said firmly. "And Fairmont knows it."

Eva looked at him, her chest tightening with a mix of gratitude and something deeper, something she could no longer deny.

"Thank you," she said softly, her voice filled with emotion.

Nathaniel's hand brushed lightly against hers, his touch grounding her. "Always," he murmured.

As they stood together in the quiet drawing room, the warmth of his presence eased the tension in her chest, reminding her that she was no longer fighting alone.

Chapter Twenty

The days following Fairmont's departure were marked by a flurry of activity. Eva threw herself into the work of revitalizing Ashcombe, her energy fueled by equal parts determination and the lingering satisfaction of standing her ground.

The tenants responded to her outreach with cautious optimism. The trial partnership with Lord Whitlock began to take shape, and Eva found herself attending meetings with landowners, laborers, and tradesmen alike. Her days were filled with the kind of purpose that left her exhausted yet fulfilled by the time the sun set.

And always, Nathaniel was there—steady, reliable, and quietly supportive. Their moments together, whether spent pouring over plans in the library or walking the estate's fields, had taken on a new intimacy, their connection deepening with each passing day.

One crisp morning, Eva stood in the manor's courtyard, watching as a group of tenants gathered near the stables. They were inspecting a newly delivered plow, its sleek metal edges gleaming in the sunlight. Nathaniel stood among them, his sleeves rolled up as he explained the benefits of the equipment.

Eva couldn't help but smile at the sight. He had a way of commanding attention without demanding it, his calm authority inspiring respect and trust.

"Admiring your steward, I see," Sophia's teasing voice broke through her thoughts.

Eva turned, her cheeks flushing slightly as she saw her sister standing nearby, her arms crossed and a mischievous grin on her face.

"Sophia," Eva said, her tone light but warning.

"Oh, don't deny it," Sophia said, stepping closer. "Anyone with eyes can see how the two of you look at each other."

Eva's blush deepened, but she held her ground. "Nathaniel has been an incredible help to Ashcombe. We're partners in this effort."

"Partners," Sophia repeated, her grin widening. "Is that what they're calling it now?"

Eva sighed, though she couldn't keep a small smile from tugging at her lips. "You're incorrigible."

"And you're in love," Sophia said softly, her teasing tone giving way to sincerity.

Eva's breath caught, and she glanced away, her chest tightening. Was it true? The thought had lingered at the edges of her mind for weeks, but hearing it spoken aloud brought it to the forefront with startling clarity.

"Don't be afraid of it, Eva," Sophia said gently. "You deserve to be happy."

Eva looked back at her sister, her expression softening. "Thank you, Sophia. Truly."

Sophia smiled, her eyes shining. "Now, go talk to him before I drag you over there myself."

Nathaniel looked up as Eva approached, his expression softening as their eyes met. The tenants, sensing the shift in his attention, offered polite nods to Eva before dispersing, leaving the two of them alone.

"Good morning," Nathaniel said, his voice warm.

"Good morning," Eva replied, her heart fluttering at the sight of him. "How's the new plow?"

"Promising," he said, gesturing to the equipment. "It should make a significant difference for the tenants, especially as we prepare for the next planting season."

Eva nodded, her gaze lingering on him. "Nathaniel... I wanted to thank you. For everything you've done—for Ashcombe, and for me."

He studied her for a moment, his hazel eyes filled with quiet intensity. "You don't need to thank me, Eva. I'm here because I want to be."

Her breath hitched, and she stepped closer, her voice trembling. "You've become more to me than I ever expected. More than I thought I deserved."

Nathaniel's expression softened, and he reached out, his hand brushing lightly against hers. "You deserve everything, Eva. And more."

The world seemed to still around them, the hum of the courtyard fading into silence as their gazes locked. Eva's heart raced, her emotions threatening to spill over.

"Nathaniel," she whispered, her voice barely audible.

Before she could say more, he stepped closer, his hand cupping her cheek with a tenderness that made her chest ache. "Eva, you've changed everything for me. You've given me hope again."

Her lips curved into a trembling smile, tears pricking at the corners of her eyes. "And you've shown me what it means to truly stand tall."

Nathaniel leaned in, his lips brushing against hers in a kiss that was soft yet filled with a quiet intensity. The warmth of his touch sent a shiver through her, and for a moment, the weight of the world fell away.

When they parted, he rested his forehead against hers, his voice low and steady. "Whatever comes next, we'll face it together."

Eva nodded, her heart swelling with emotion. "Together."

The afternoon passed in a blur of activity, but the memory of their moment lingered, a steady flame burning in Eva's chest. She moved through her tasks with a newfound sense of purpose, her steps lighter and her resolve stronger than ever.

That evening, as the household gathered for supper, the mood felt warmer, less strained. Sophia chattered animatedly about her latest plans for the garden, while their father listened with a faint smile. Even Lady Margaret seemed less severe, though she said little.

As the meal concluded, Eva stood, addressing the room with quiet confidence. "I have something I'd like to say."

All eyes turned to her, the quiet hum of conversation falling silent.

"I know the past months have been difficult," Eva began, her gaze sweeping across the table. "And I know my decisions have caused tension, particularly between Mother and me. But I believe we're finally moving toward something better—for Ashcombe and for all of us."

Margaret's expression remained unreadable, but Sophia beamed, her pride evident.

"I want to thank all of you," Eva continued, her voice steady. "For your patience, your support, and your faith in this effort. Together, we're building something that will last."

As she sat back down, the quiet that followed was filled not with tension but with a sense of unity—a feeling Eva hadn't realized she had been longing for.

Later that night, as she stood by the window of her room, gazing out at the moonlit garden, Eva felt a quiet sense of peace settle over her. The path ahead was still uncertain, but for the first time, she wasn't afraid.

Nathaniel's words echoed in her mind, a steady refrain that buoyed her spirits. Whatever came next, she knew she wouldn't face it alone.

And for now, that was enough.

Chapter Twenty-One

The crisp dawn air carried the scent of freshly turned earth and the faint tang of dew. Eva stood on the veranda, her hands wrapped around a steaming cup of tea as she watched the estate come to life. The tenants were already at work in the fields, their figures moving with practiced efficiency as the first rays of sunlight stretched across the land.

It was a sight that should have filled her with pride and satisfaction. Yet, a sense of unease gnawed at the edges of her thoughts, a reminder that Ashcombe's fragile progress was far from guaranteed.

Nathaniel found her there an hour later, his boots crunching softly against the gravel as he approached. His presence was grounding, the quiet strength in his gaze a welcome counterbalance to her restless thoughts.

"Couldn't sleep?" he asked, stopping beside her.

"I slept," Eva replied, though her tone lacked conviction. "I just couldn't stay in bed."

Nathaniel studied her for a moment, then gestured toward the fields. "Walk with me."

She nodded, setting her cup down on the veranda's railing before falling into step beside him.

They walked in companionable silence, the morning sounds of the estate—a horse's soft nicker, the distant laughter of children—creating a soothing backdrop. As they reached the edge of the fields, Nathaniel stopped, turning to face her.

"What's on your mind?" he asked, his tone gentle but direct.

Eva hesitated, her gaze drifting to the horizon. "Everything," she admitted. "The estate, the tenants, my mother... Fairmont."

Nathaniel's expression darkened slightly at the mention of Fairmont, but he said nothing, waiting for her to continue.

"I feel like we're making progress," Eva said, her voice soft. "But it's so precarious. One wrong step, and everything we've worked for could come undone."

Nathaniel reached out, his hand brushing lightly against hers. "You've built something stronger than you realize, Eva. The tenants believe in you. Whitlock believes in you. And so do I."

Her breath caught, the warmth of his touch grounding her. "I don't know what I would do without you," she said softly.

"You won't have to find out," Nathaniel replied, his voice steady. "Whatever happens, I'll be here."

Their conversation was interrupted by the sound of approaching footsteps. They turned to see Mr. Cartwright hurrying toward them, a sheaf of papers clutched in his hand.

"My lady," Cartwright called, his expression unusually animated. "You'll want to see this."

Eva and Nathaniel exchanged a glance before following Cartwright back toward the manor.

In the study, Cartwright spread the papers out on the desk, his finger pointing to a ledger entry. "These are the most recent accounts from the tenants," he explained. "And this—" he tapped another sheet "—is a record of the initial crop yields since implementing the new plow and rotation methods."

Eva leaned over the desk, her eyes scanning the numbers. As the data sank in, a smile broke across her face.

"It's working," she said, her voice filled with quiet amazement.

"It's more than working," Cartwright said with a rare note of enthusiasm. "If these trends hold, we could see a surplus by the next season."

Nathaniel's lips curved into a faint smile. "That's excellent news."

Eva straightened, her chest swelling with a mix of relief and pride. "It's just the beginning, but it's a beginning."

Cartwright nodded. "I'll continue monitoring the progress closely. For now, I thought you'd like to know that your efforts are bearing fruit—quite literally."

"Thank you, Mr. Cartwright," Eva said, her gratitude genuine.

As Cartwright excused himself, Eva turned to Nathaniel, her smile soft but radiant. "This wouldn't have been possible without you."

He shook his head. "It's your vision, Eva. I'm just helping you bring it to life."

Her chest tightened at his words, the sincerity in his gaze making her heart ache in the best possible way.

The sense of accomplishment carried Eva through the rest of the day. She spent hours in the fields, speaking with tenants and workers, listening to their concerns and offering encouragement. The work was exhausting, but it filled her with a sense of purpose she hadn't felt in years.

By the time she returned to the manor, the sun was dipping below the horizon, casting the estate in hues of orange and gold. She made her way to the drawing room, where Sophia was curled up on the settee with a book.

"You look like you've had quite the day," Sophia said, setting the book aside.

"I have," Eva replied, sinking into a nearby chair.

Sophia studied her for a moment, her expression thoughtful. "You're happier, Eva. It suits you."

Eva smiled faintly, her thoughts drifting to Nathaniel. "I think I'm finally starting to feel like myself again."

Sophia's grin widened. "And does a certain Captain Grey have anything to do with that?"

Eva laughed softly, shaking her head. "You're impossible."

"I'm observant," Sophia corrected, her tone light but knowing.

Eva's smile lingered as she leaned back in her chair, her heart lighter than it had been in months.

That evening, as she sat in her room, Eva reflected on the day's events. The progress they had made, the support of the tenants, and the quiet strength she drew from Nathaniel's presence—it all felt like pieces of a puzzle finally falling into place.

She glanced out the window, the garden bathed in moonlight. The path ahead was still uncertain, but for the first time, she felt truly prepared to face it.

And she knew she wouldn't be facing it alone.

Chapter Twenty-Two

The first hints of autumn's chill whispered through the morning air as Eva stood on the terrace, watching the estate stir to life. She wrapped her shawl tighter around her shoulders, the fabric a soft barrier against the brisk breeze. The promise of change hung heavy in the air—not just in the shifting seasons, but in the subtle but unmistakable progress Ashcombe was beginning to see.

Nathaniel found her there, his presence quiet but steady. She turned at the sound of his boots against the flagstones, her lips curving into a faint smile.

"Good morning," she said.

"Morning," he replied, his gaze sweeping over her with quiet concern. "You're up early."

"I couldn't sleep," Eva admitted, though there was no weariness in her voice. "The tenants' meeting is today, and I suppose my mind is too busy thinking about what might come of it."

Nathaniel nodded, stepping closer. "You've done the work, Eva. They've seen it. And they trust you."

Her smile softened, her chest tightening at the quiet confidence in his voice. "I hope you're right."

"I am," he said simply, his tone leaving no room for doubt.

The meeting was held in the great hall, its high ceilings and tall windows lending an air of formality to the gathering. The tenants arrived in groups, their chatter a mixture of curiosity and cautious optimism.

Eva stood near the head of the room, Nathaniel at her side, as the last of the attendees filed in. She smoothed her skirts with trembling hands, the weight of their expectations pressing heavily on her chest.

Nathaniel leaned in slightly, his voice low and reassuring. "You've got this."

Eva took a deep breath, nodding as she stepped forward to address the crowd.

"Thank you all for coming," she began, her voice steady despite the rapid beat of her heart. "I know the past few months have been difficult—for all of us. But I believe that together, we've begun to lay the foundation for something better."

She paused, her gaze sweeping over the room. The tenants were listening intently, their faces a mixture of skepticism and hope.

"The changes we've made so far are only the beginning," Eva continued. "With your support, we can build an Ashcombe that thrives—not just for today, but for generations to come. But it will require trust, effort, and a willingness to embrace new ways of thinking."

One of the older tenants, Mr. Harding, stepped forward, his weathered face creased with thought. "And what guarantee do we have that this plan will work, my lady? We've heard promises before."

Eva met his gaze, her expression earnest. "I can't offer guarantees, Mr. Harding. But I can promise you this: I will work as hard as any of you to see this plan succeed. And I will listen—to your concerns, your ideas, and your needs. This is not just my estate—it's our community."

A murmur of agreement rippled through the crowd, and Eva felt her confidence grow.

Another tenant, a younger man named Thomas, raised his hand. "What about the new plows and tools, my lady? Will there be enough to go around?"

Nathaniel stepped forward, his voice calm but authoritative. "The new equipment is being distributed based on the fields' needs and the crop schedules we've developed. Everyone will benefit in time, but we'll need to work together to ensure it's done fairly."

Thomas nodded, seemingly satisfied with the answer.

As more questions were asked and answered, the mood in the room began to shift. The initial skepticism gave way to cautious optimism, and by the end of the meeting, Eva felt a spark of hope ignite within her.

As the tenants dispersed, their conversations carrying an air of tentative excitement, Eva turned to Nathaniel, her chest swelling with relief.

"That went better than I expected," she said softly.

"You were incredible," Nathaniel replied, his gaze filled with quiet pride.

Eva's cheeks flushed, but she couldn't help the smile that spread across her face. "Thank you. For everything."

Nathaniel shook his head. "This is your victory, Eva. I'm just here to make sure you see it through."

Her heart swelled at his words, and she reached out, her hand brushing lightly against his. "I don't know what I'd do without you."

"You won't have to find out," he said, his voice steady.

For a moment, they stood in silence, the connection between them unspoken but undeniable. Then Sophia's voice rang out, breaking the moment.

"Well, that was something!" she said, striding into the hall with her usual energy. "You had them hanging on your every word, Eva."

Eva turned, laughing softly at her sister's enthusiasm. "It's a start."

"It's more than that," Sophia said, her smile wide. "It's a triumph."

Nathaniel chuckled, his tone teasing. "She's not wrong."

Eva shook her head, though her smile lingered. "We still have a long way to go."

"And you'll get there," Sophia said confidently. "With Captain Grey at your side, how could you not?"

Eva's blush deepened, but she didn't deny it.

That evening, as the household settled into the quiet rhythm of dusk, Eva found herself back in the garden. The roses swayed gently in the cool breeze, their petals pale in the moonlight.

Nathaniel joined her there, his presence as steady and comforting as ever. They stood in silence for a while, the weight of the day settling over them like a soft blanket.

"You've changed this place," Nathaniel said finally, his voice quiet but filled with admiration.

Eva turned to him, her chest tightening. "We've changed it. Together."

He smiled, his gaze warm. "And we're just getting started."

As the moonlight cast a silvery glow over the garden, Eva felt a quiet sense of certainty settle within her. The path ahead would be difficult, but it was one she was ready to walk—hand in hand with the man who had become her anchor, her partner, and her love.

Chapter Twenty-Three

A week later, the first of the autumn storms rolled in, blanketing Ashcombe in a cold, persistent rain. The fields, once golden under the late summer sun, were now dark with mud, their furrows gleaming under the weight of water. The tenants worked tirelessly to secure their crops against the weather, and Eva was among them, her skirts caked with dirt and her hair damp under the hood of her cloak.

She had insisted on being present, her hands as busy as anyone else's. The sight of her laboring alongside them inspired the tenants in a way no speech could, their appreciation evident in the grateful nods and murmured thanks she received.

"You'll catch your death out here," Nathaniel said as he approached, his own coat drenched.

Eva glanced up from the sack of potatoes she was securing, her cheeks flushed with cold. "And you won't?" she retorted, though her tone was light.

Nathaniel's lips twitched into a faint smile. "Touché. But you've done enough for today. Go inside, warm yourself. I'll handle the rest."

Eva straightened, brushing a strand of wet hair from her face. "You're not dismissing me from my own fields, Captain Grey."

He arched an eyebrow, though the corners of his eyes crinkled with amusement. "As you wish, my lady. But at least let me carry that for you."

Before she could protest, he hoisted the heavy sack over his shoulder with ease, his strength a quiet reminder of the steady presence he had become in her life.

By the time the rain eased and the last of the work was done, twilight had settled over the estate. Eva returned to the manor exhausted but satisfied, her body aching from the day's exertion.

Sophia met her at the door, her expression equal parts exasperated and amused. "You look like you've been wrestling in the mud," she said, eyeing Eva's sodden cloak and boots.

"I may as well have been," Eva replied with a weary laugh. "But the fields are secure."

Sophia shook her head, though her smile softened. "You're impossible, Eva. Now, go change before you frighten the staff."

An hour later, freshly bathed and dressed in a warm wool gown, Eva made her way to the library. The fire crackled in the hearth, casting a golden glow over the room's dark wood and well-worn books.

Nathaniel was already there, a cup of tea in his hands as he stood by the fire. He looked up as she entered, his expression softening.

"You clean up well," he teased, his tone warm.

Eva smiled, sinking into the armchair opposite him. "And you somehow look exactly the same as you did in the fields."

He chuckled, setting his cup down on the mantel. "It's a talent."

They lapsed into comfortable silence, the warmth of the fire easing the lingering chill in Eva's bones.

"You did good today," Nathaniel said after a while, his voice quiet.

"So did you," Eva replied, her gaze meeting his.

He leaned against the mantel, his hazel eyes thoughtful. "The tenants trust you, Eva. They see how much you care, how hard you're willing to work for them. That kind of leadership—it's rare."

Her chest tightened at his words, a mix of pride and gratitude swelling within her. "I couldn't have done any of this without you," she said softly.

Nathaniel shook his head. "You give me too much credit. This is your vision, Eva. I'm just here to help you see it through."

She stood, crossing the room to stand beside him. The firelight danced in his eyes as she looked up at him, her heart pounding. "You've been my anchor, Nathaniel. My partner. And... my friend."

He reached out, his hand brushing lightly against hers. "And you've been mine," he said, his voice steady but filled with emotion.

Eva's breath caught, the air between them charged with unspoken feelings. She took a step closer, her hand resting against his chest. "I'm not afraid anymore," she whispered.

Nathaniel's hand came up to cup her cheek, his touch warm and grounding. "Neither am I," he murmured.

The kiss that followed was soft and slow, filled with a quiet intensity that left Eva breathless. It was a promise, unspoken but deeply felt—a vow of partnership, of support, and of love.

When they parted, Nathaniel rested his forehead against hers, his voice barely above a whisper. "We'll face whatever comes next. Together."

Eva smiled, her chest swelling with a sense of peace she hadn't felt in years. "Together."

The storm continued to rage outside, but inside the library, the world felt quiet and still. As Eva and Nathaniel stood by the fire, the weight of the past weeks seemed to lift, replaced by the certainty of their shared path.

And for the first time, Eva felt that the future—uncertain and daunting as it was—was something she could face with courage and hope.

Chapter Twenty-Four

The next morning, the storm had passed, leaving the estate drenched in golden sunlight. The rain had washed the fields clean, the air crisp with the scent of damp earth and fresh grass. Eva stepped onto the veranda, the warmth of the morning a stark contrast to the cold wind of the previous day.

Her heart felt light, buoyed by the memory of her quiet moment with Nathaniel in the library. The tenderness they had shared had been a revelation, a confirmation of the bond that had grown between them.

But as the sunlight streamed over Ashcombe, Eva knew the day would bring new challenges. With the fields secure, her attention turned to the tenants' growing concerns about Lord Fairmont. His presence lingered in their minds like a shadow, a reminder of his meddling and the unspoken threats he had made.

By midday, Eva was in the study with Nathaniel, the large oak desk between them piled high with letters, estate accounts, and reports from the tenants. Mr. Cartwright had just delivered the latest financial updates and excused himself, leaving Eva and Nathaniel to sift through the information.

Nathaniel leaned over the desk, his brow furrowed as he examined one of the ledgers. "Fairmont's influence is waning, but he's not gone yet," he said, his tone measured.

Eva sighed, brushing a strand of hair from her face. "I know. And I hate that he still holds even a sliver of power here. But what more can we do?"

Nathaniel straightened, his hazel eyes meeting hers. "We keep going. Whitlock's partnership is solid, and the tenants trust you more every day. Fairmont's strength lies in intimidation, but without the community's support, he has no real power."

Eva nodded, his words bolstering her resolve. "You're right. He's losing ground, and we need to make sure he can't regain it."

She picked up one of the letters, her gaze scanning the contents. It was from Lord Whitlock, offering updates on their shared plans and proposing a meeting to finalize their next steps.

"Whitlock wants to meet," she said, passing the letter to Nathaniel.

He skimmed the page, nodding. "Good. Solidifying his involvement will show the tenants—and Fairmont—that you're serious about this new path for Ashcombe."

Eva smiled faintly, a flicker of hope sparking in her chest. "Then let's arrange it."

The meeting with Whitlock was set for three days later, and the days leading up to it were filled with preparation. Eva worked tirelessly, drafting proposals and gathering information to present. Nathaniel was by her side throughout, his steady presence a constant source of support.

Sophia, ever eager to help, took it upon herself to manage the household in Eva's absence, ensuring that every detail was attended to.

"You'll do brilliantly," Sophia said as she adjusted the collar of Eva's riding coat on the morning of the meeting.

Eva smiled, her nerves tempered by her sister's enthusiasm. "Thank you, Sophia. For everything."

"Just don't let Whitlock see you doubt yourself," Sophia replied with a grin. "You've already won him over—you just have to remind him why."

Whitlock Manor was a picture of autumnal charm when they arrived, its ivy-covered walls bathed in warm sunlight. Lord Whitlock greeted them in the drawing room, his demeanor as affable as ever.

"Lady Ashcombe," he said, extending a hand. "Captain Grey. It's good to see you both."

"Thank you for meeting with us," Eva replied, shaking his hand.

"Of course," Whitlock said, gesturing for them to sit. "I must say, your letters have been quite persuasive. And your progress—well, it's nothing short of impressive."

Eva felt a swell of pride, though she kept her expression calm. "Thank you, my lord. But there's still much to do, and I believe that working together will benefit us both."

Whitlock nodded, his expression thoughtful. "Your vision for Ashcombe is bold, Lady Ashcombe. And I admire your determination to see it through. Tell me—how do you plan to sustain this progress long-term?"

Eva glanced at Nathaniel, drawing strength from his steady presence before turning back to Whitlock. "By building a foundation of trust and collaboration," she said. "The tenants are already seeing the benefits of the changes we've implemented. If we continue to reinvest in the land and the people, I believe we can create a community that thrives."

Whitlock leaned back in his chair, a faint smile playing on his lips. "You're a remarkable woman, Lady Ashcombe. It's not often I meet someone so willing to take risks for the sake of others."

Eva's cheeks flushed, but she held his gaze. "I've had good guidance," she said, glancing at Nathaniel.

Whitlock's smile widened. "Then I see no reason not to move forward. Let's formalize our partnership and ensure that Ashcombe's future is as bright as you envision."

The ride back to Ashcombe was quiet, the weight of the meeting settling over Eva like a warm cloak. She felt a sense of accomplishment she hadn't known she was capable of, her confidence growing with each small victory.

"You were extraordinary," Nathaniel said, breaking the silence.

Eva smiled, her chest tightening at the warmth in his voice. "I couldn't have done it without you."

He shook his head, his gaze soft. "You've done more than you realize, Eva. And you're just getting started."

As they approached the manor, the first lights of evening flickered to life in the windows, casting a golden glow over the estate.

Eva glanced at Nathaniel, her heart swelling with gratitude and something deeper, something that felt like hope.

"Thank you," she said softly.

He smiled, his expression filled with quiet certainty. "Always."

Chapter Twenty-Five

The next few weeks passed in a blur of progress and small victories. The partnership with Lord Whitlock had begun in earnest, and the first shipment of shared resources arrived at Ashcombe amid a flurry of excitement from the tenants. The new tools, seed varieties, and plows were distributed carefully, ensuring that each field received what it needed most.

Nathaniel oversaw the allocation with his usual calm efficiency, working alongside the tenants to demonstrate the proper use of the new equipment. Eva remained ever-present, her hands as busy as her mind, offering reassurance and direction to those who were still hesitant about the changes.

By mid-October, the estate began to show the first signs of its transformation. Crops planted using the new methods were thriving, their vibrant green shoots a hopeful contrast to the gray skies of autumn. The tenants, though cautious, began to express their optimism more openly, their conversations punctuated with cautious laughter and the occasional joke.

One chilly afternoon, Eva found herself in the stables, her fingers brushing over the sleek flank of her horse as she prepared for a ride. She hadn't ventured far from the estate in weeks, her days consumed with the relentless demands of the plan she and Nathaniel had forged.

As she adjusted the saddle, she heard the familiar sound of boots on the stable floor. She turned to see Nathaniel approaching, his coat dusted with hay and his hair slightly tousled from the wind.

"Going somewhere?" he asked, a teasing lilt in his voice.

Eva smiled faintly, brushing a strand of hair from her face. "Just for a short ride. I needed some air."

"Mind if I join you?" he asked, already reaching for his own horse.

"I'd like that," Eva said, her voice soft but warm.

The countryside was a patchwork of muted greens and browns, the rolling hills dotted with patches of golden leaves that clung stubbornly to the trees. The air was crisp, carrying the faint scent of wood smoke from the village chimneys below.

Eva and Nathaniel rode in companionable silence for a while, the sound of their horses' hooves muffled against the soft earth. The tension that had clung to Eva for so long began to ease, replaced by a quiet sense of peace.

"Have you thought about what's next?" Nathaniel asked after a while, his tone casual but curious.

Eva glanced at him, her brow furrowing slightly. "Next?"

"For Ashcombe," he clarified. "You've made incredible progress, but this is just the beginning."

She nodded, her gaze drifting to the horizon. "I think about it all the time. There's so much more I want to do—for the tenants, for the estate. But sometimes it feels... overwhelming."

Nathaniel's lips curved into a faint smile. "That's because you care. And because you're trying to do something extraordinary."

His words sent a warm rush through her chest, and she looked at him, her expression softening. "You make it sound so simple."

"It's not," he said, his gaze steady. "But that's what makes it worth it."

Eva smiled, a quiet determination settling over her. "Then I suppose we'll just have to keep going."

"We will," Nathaniel said, his voice filled with quiet certainty.

As they returned to the estate, the familiar sight of the manor came into view, its stone walls gleaming faintly in the fading light. The sight filled Eva with a renewed sense of purpose, a reminder of all they had accomplished and all that remained to be done.

Sophia met them in the courtyard, her cheeks flushed from the cold. She waved excitedly as they dismounted, her voice carrying easily across the crisp air.

"There you are! I was beginning to think you'd ridden off for good," she teased.

Eva laughed softly, handing her reins to a waiting stable hand. "Not quite. What's happened while we were gone?"

Sophia's grin widened. "You received another letter—from Lord Whitlock. He says he's been hearing good things from the tenants and wants to meet again to discuss expanding the partnership."

Eva's chest tightened with a mix of excitement and apprehension. "That's wonderful news."

"It is," Sophia agreed, her eyes sparkling. "And it's all thanks to you."

Eva glanced at Nathaniel, her heart swelling with gratitude. "Thanks to all of us," she said softly.

That evening, Eva sat in the drawing room, the letter from Lord Whitlock spread out before her. The fire crackled softly in the hearth, its warmth a welcome contrast to the chill that seeped through the manor's stone walls.

Nathaniel entered quietly, his presence as steadying as ever. He crossed the room to stand beside her, his gaze flicking to the letter.

"Good news?" he asked.

Eva nodded, a small smile playing on her lips. "Whitlock wants to expand the partnership. It's more than I'd hoped for."

Nathaniel leaned against the edge of the desk, his expression thoughtful. "And it's well-earned. You've worked for this, Eva."

She looked up at him, her heart tightening at the warmth in his gaze. "We've worked for this," she corrected gently.

His lips curved into a faint smile, and he reached out, his hand brushing lightly against hers. "You've changed this place, Eva. And you've changed me."

Her breath caught, the sincerity in his voice cutting through her. "Nathaniel..."

He shook his head, his gaze steady. "I don't know what the future holds, but I know I want to face it with you."

Tears pricked at her eyes, and she nodded, her voice trembling as she replied. "I feel the same."

As the fire crackled softly behind them, Eva felt a quiet sense of certainty settle over her. The path ahead was still uncertain, but she knew they would face it together.

Chapter Twenty-Six

The days leading up to the next meeting with Lord Whitlock were filled with a mix of nervous anticipation and relentless preparation. The tenants were cautiously optimistic, their initial doubts about the partnership easing as the benefits of the new methods became evident.

Eva spent long hours drafting proposals and reviewing financial records, her determination to present Ashcombe as a beacon of progress driving her forward. Nathaniel was ever by her side, his quiet support and practical wisdom steadying her when the weight of her responsibilities threatened to overwhelm her.

The morning of the meeting dawned crisp and bright, the kind of autumn day that seemed to promise possibility. Eva dressed carefully, her attire chosen to strike a balance between practicality and poise. As Sophia fastened the last button on her riding coat, she offered a conspiratorial grin.

"You look every bit the lady of the manor," Sophia said. "Fairmont would probably faint if he saw you like this."

Eva rolled her eyes, though a smile tugged at her lips. "Fairmont has no say in anything I do anymore. And I intend to keep it that way."

"Good," Sophia said, her tone firm. "Because Ashcombe is thriving, and you're the reason why. Don't let anyone make you doubt that."

Eva hugged her sister tightly, her heart swelling with gratitude. "Thank you, Sophia. For always believing in me."

"Always," Sophia replied, her voice soft.

The ride to Whitlock Manor was brisk, the chill in the air offset by the warmth of the sun. Nathaniel rode beside Eva, his presence a quiet reassurance.

"Are you ready?" he asked as they approached the gates.

Eva nodded, her gaze steady. "I think so. This meeting is important—not just for the partnership, but for the tenants' trust in me."

"They already trust you," Nathaniel said. "Today is about showing them—and Whitlock—that their faith is well-placed."

His words bolstered her confidence, and as they dismounted and entered the manor, Eva felt a renewed sense of purpose.

Lord Whitlock greeted them in the drawing room, his demeanor as warm and affable as ever. The fire crackled in the hearth, casting a golden glow over the richly appointed space.

"Lady Ashcombe, Captain Grey," Whitlock said, gesturing for them to sit. "It's good to see you both again."

"Thank you for meeting with us, my lord," Eva replied, her tone poised.

"I've been hearing good things about Ashcombe," Whitlock said, pouring tea for each of them. "Your tenants speak highly of the changes you've implemented. It's no small feat to win over a skeptical community."

Eva smiled, a flicker of pride warming her chest. "They've been willing to adapt because they see the potential for a better future. And your support has been instrumental in making that possible."

Whitlock inclined his head, his expression thoughtful. "You've proven yourself a formidable leader, Lady Ashcombe. And your vision for the estate is both ambitious and admirable."

He leaned forward slightly, his gaze intent. "Tell me—what are your long-term goals for Ashcombe? Beyond the immediate improvements?"

Eva glanced at Nathaniel, drawing strength from his steady presence, before turning back to Whitlock. "I want Ashcombe to be a model for sustainable growth," she said. "A place where tenants and landowners work together to create prosperity for everyone. I believe that by investing in people as much as the land, we can build a community that thrives for generations."

Whitlock's smile widened, and he nodded slowly. "It's a bold vision. And I believe it's one worth pursuing."

Eva's chest tightened with relief and excitement. "Thank you, my lord. Your continued partnership would mean everything to us."

Whitlock reached for a nearby ledger, flipping through its pages. "Let's formalize the expansion, then. Additional resources, shared labor initiatives, and perhaps even a trial exchange program for our tenants to learn from each other's methods."

Nathaniel leaned forward, his voice calm but enthusiastic. "That's an excellent idea, my lord. The tenants would benefit greatly from shared knowledge and experiences."

Whitlock smiled. "Then it's settled. Lady Ashcombe, Captain Grey, you've earned my full support."

The ride back to Ashcombe was filled with a quiet sense of triumph. The partnership had not only been solidified but expanded, and Eva felt a new wave of hope for the future.

As the manor came into view, she turned to Nathaniel, her heart swelling with gratitude. "Thank you," she said softly.

He arched an eyebrow, his lips curving into a faint smile. "For what?"

"For everything," she replied. "For standing by me, for believing in this vision, and for helping me make it a reality."

Nathaniel's gaze softened, and he reached out, his hand brushing lightly against hers. "It's not just your vision, Eva. It's ours. And I'll be here for as long as you'll have me."

Her breath caught, and she smiled, her voice trembling with emotion. "Then you'll be here forever."

His smile widened, and he squeezed her hand gently. "Forever it is."

That evening, the household gathered for supper, the mood light and celebratory. Sophia regaled them with tales from the village, her laughter infectious as she animatedly described the antics of the local children. Even Lady Margaret seemed more subdued, her sharp edges softened by the unmistakable signs of progress around her.

After the meal, Eva found herself in the library with Nathaniel once again. The fire crackled softly in the hearth, and the room was filled with the comforting scent of aged leather and wood smoke.

As they reviewed the notes from the day's meeting, Eva leaned back in her chair, her gaze drifting to Nathaniel. "Do you ever think about the future?" she asked softly.

He glanced up, his brow furrowing slightly. "I think about it all the time."

"And what do you see?" she pressed, her voice barely above a whisper.

Nathaniel hesitated, his gaze steady as he met hers. "I see a place that's thriving. A place where people feel safe and valued. And I see you, Eva—leading it all with that fire in your heart."

Her chest tightened, and she looked away, her cheeks flushing. "You make it sound so simple."

"It's not," he said, his voice soft. "But nothing worth having ever is."

Eva smiled, a quiet sense of certainty settling over her. The future remained uncertain, but she knew one thing for sure: whatever came next, she wouldn't face it alone.

Chapter Twenty-Seven

The turning leaves of late October painted the Ashcombe estate in hues of gold and crimson, the vibrant colors a stark contrast to the chill in the air. The tenants had settled into the rhythm of the new methods, and the estate hummed with the quiet productivity of a community working together.

But not all was peaceful. The lingering specter of Lord Fairmont loomed over Eva's thoughts, his parting words a constant reminder that his interference was far from over.

One morning, as Eva stood in the garden reviewing notes from the latest tenant reports, Nathaniel approached, his stride purposeful but his expression cautious.

"There's something you need to see," he said, his tone low.

Eva frowned, folding the papers and tucking them into the pocket of her coat. "What is it?"

He hesitated for a moment before gesturing toward the fields. "It's easier to show you."

They walked together in silence, the crisp air filled with the faint rustle of leaves and the distant sound of tenants working. When they reached the edge of the eastern fields, Eva's breath caught.

Several sections of fencing had been torn down, the posts splintered and the wire twisted beyond repair. A portion of the crop, which had been nearing harvest, lay trampled and ruined.

"Who would do this?" Eva whispered, her voice trembling with anger and disbelief.

Nathaniel's jaw tightened, his gaze scanning the damage. "It's no accident. Someone wanted this to happen."

"Fairmont," Eva said, the name leaving her lips like a curse.

Nathaniel nodded grimly. "It's possible. He's been quiet since his last visit—too quiet. This kind of sabotage feels like his way of sending a message."

Eva's hands curled into fists at her sides, her chest burning with fury. "He's trying to intimidate us. To make us doubt ourselves. But I won't let him win."

Nathaniel placed a steadying hand on her arm, his voice calm but firm. "We'll fix this, Eva. But we need to be smart about it. If this is Fairmont's doing, we have to tread carefully."

She met his gaze, her anger tempered by his quiet strength. "You're right. Let's start by repairing the damage and ensuring the tenants feel safe. Then we'll decide how to handle Fairmont."

The repairs began immediately, with tenants and workers rallying together under Nathaniel's direction. Eva worked alongside them, her hands blistered and her skirts dusted with dirt as she helped reset the broken posts and clear the ruined crops.

The atmosphere was tense, the tenants murmuring about the sabotage and the possibility of further attacks. But Eva's presence seemed to steady them, her determination a quiet reassurance.

As the sun dipped below the horizon, casting the fields in shades of amber and purple, Nathaniel called a halt to the day's work.

"Let's finish the rest tomorrow," he said, his voice carrying across the field. "You've all done enough for one day."

The workers dispersed, their exhaustion evident but their spirits bolstered by the progress they had made.

Eva lingered, her gaze sweeping over the repaired sections of fencing. "It's a start," she said softly.

Nathaniel stepped beside her, his presence grounding. "It's more than that. You showed them that you're willing to fight for this place. That matters."

Her chest tightened at his words, and she turned to him, her voice trembling with emotion. "Thank you, Nathaniel. For always being here. For standing with me."

He reached out, his hand brushing lightly against hers. "You don't have to thank me, Eva. This is as much my fight as it is yours."

Her breath caught, the warmth of his touch grounding her even as her thoughts raced. "I couldn't do this without you," she whispered.

Nathaniel's gaze softened, and he squeezed her hand gently. "And you'll never have to."

That night, as Eva sat by the fire in the library, her thoughts churned with plans and possibilities. The sabotage was a stark reminder of how precarious their progress was, but it also fueled her resolve.

Sophia entered quietly, her usual exuberance tempered by concern. "I heard about the fields," she said, taking the chair across from Eva.

Eva nodded, her expression grim. "It was deliberate. Someone's trying to undermine everything we've worked for."

Sophia's brow furrowed, and she leaned forward. "Fairmont?"

"Most likely," Eva replied. "But I won't let him win, Sophia. Ashcombe is stronger than his petty schemes."

Sophia smiled faintly, pride shining in her eyes. "That's the Eva I know."

They sat in silence for a moment, the firelight casting flickering shadows across the room.

"Do you ever think about leaving?" Sophia asked suddenly, her voice soft.

Eva blinked, startled by the question. "Leaving?"

Sophia shrugged, her gaze thoughtful. "Starting over somewhere new. Somewhere far away from Fairmont and all the expectations that come with this place."

Eva considered the idea, her heart aching at the thought of abandoning Ashcombe. "I've thought about it," she admitted. "But I could never leave. This is my home, Sophia. It's worth fighting for."

Sophia nodded, her smile bittersweet. "I thought you'd say that. And you're right—Ashcombe wouldn't be the same without you."

As the household settled into the quiet rhythms of the night, Eva felt a renewed sense of purpose. The road ahead would be fraught with challenges, but she knew she wasn't walking it alone.

And for now, that was enough.

Chapter Twenty-Eight

The following morning dawned gray and cold, the clouds hanging low over Ashcombe as if mirroring the tension that gripped the estate. News of the sabotage had spread quickly, and while the tenants remained committed to the repairs, a quiet unease had settled over them.

Eva was determined to address the matter directly. After breakfast, she gathered the tenants and workers in the great hall, her resolve firm despite the anxious whispers that filled the room.

Nathaniel stood beside her, his steady presence a silent reassurance as she stepped forward to address the crowd.

"I know many of you are worried," Eva began, her voice calm but strong. "And I won't pretend that what happened wasn't deliberate. Someone is trying to undermine what we've built here."

A murmur of agreement rippled through the room, and Eva continued, her gaze sweeping over the gathered faces.

"But let me be clear: we will not be intimidated. Ashcombe is stronger than this, and so are we. Together, we've already accomplished so much—and together, we will overcome this, too."

The murmurs grew louder, shifting from uncertainty to quiet determination.

Mr. Harding, the elder tenant who had voiced skepticism during their earlier meetings, stepped forward. His weathered face was creased with thought, but his eyes held a spark of resolve.

"You've stood with us, my lady," Harding said, his voice carrying across the room. "We'll stand with you, too. Whatever it takes."

A chorus of agreement followed, and Eva felt a swell of gratitude and pride.

"Thank you," she said, her voice trembling slightly. "Your trust means everything to me. And I promise you—I won't let you down."

As the tenants dispersed, their spirits visibly lifted, Eva turned to Nathaniel, her chest tight with emotion.

"Do you think they believe me?" she asked softly.

Nathaniel smiled, his hazel eyes warm. "They don't just believe you, Eva. They trust you. And that's more powerful than anything Fairmont could ever throw at us."

Her lips curved into a faint smile, though the weight of the situation still pressed heavily on her. "I just hope I can live up to that trust."

"You already have," Nathaniel said, his tone firm.

The next few days were consumed by efforts to secure the estate against further attacks. Nathaniel organized patrols to monitor the fields and surrounding areas, while Eva worked closely with Mr. Cartwright to ensure the repairs were completed quickly and efficiently.

Sophia, ever eager to help, busied herself in the village, rallying additional support from local tradesmen and farmers. Her charm and enthusiasm proved invaluable, and by the week's end, Ashcombe's defenses were stronger than ever.

One evening, as Eva and Nathaniel walked the perimeter of the estate, the faint glow of lanterns illuminated the repaired fencing. The air was cold and still, the quiet broken only by the soft crunch of their boots against the frosted ground.

"You've done a remarkable thing here," Nathaniel said, his voice low.

Eva glanced at him, her breath visible in the chilly air. "We've done it together."

He smiled faintly, his gaze steady. "You're too modest, Eva. The tenants see you as their leader because you've earned it. You've shown them what's possible."

Her cheeks flushed, though whether from the cold or his words, she couldn't tell. "I couldn't have done any of this without you, Nathaniel. You've been my strength when I doubted myself."

His expression softened, and he stopped, turning to face her fully. "And you've been mine. You've reminded me what it means to believe in something again."

Eva's heart swelled, the warmth of his words cutting through the cold night air. She reached out, her fingers brushing lightly against his. "I don't know what the future holds," she said softly, "but I know I want to face it with you."

Nathaniel's hand closed around hers, his grip firm but gentle. "Then let's face it together."

For a moment, the world seemed to fade away, leaving only the quiet connection between them.

The quiet didn't last long.

As they returned to the manor, a rider approached at a gallop, his horse's hooves kicking up clouds of dirt and frost. Eva's pulse quickened as the rider reined in sharply, his face pale and strained.

"My lady," the rider said, his voice breathless. "You need to come quickly. There's been an incident in the village."

Eva's heart sank, and she exchanged a glance with Nathaniel, his expression darkening.

"What happened?" she asked, her voice steady despite the knot of dread in her chest.

"Fairmont," the rider said grimly. "He's stirring trouble with the tradesmen—trying to turn them against you."

Eva straightened, her resolve hardening. "Thank you for telling me. I'll be there immediately."

Nathaniel stepped forward, his tone firm. "I'm coming with you."

She nodded, her gratitude for his unwavering support silent but deeply felt.

The village square was a hive of activity when they arrived, the air thick with tension. A small crowd had gathered, their voices raised in angry debate. At the center of the commotion stood Lord Fairmont, his polished boots gleaming in the lantern light as he addressed the tradesmen with smooth, calculated charm.

"Lady Ashcombe's plans may seem noble," Fairmont was saying, his tone oozing with false concern. "But mark my words—they will lead to ruin. The costs will fall on your shoulders, and your livelihoods will suffer for it."

Eva's fury flared, but she kept her expression calm as she stepped forward, her voice cutting through the noise like a blade. "That's enough, Lord Fairmont."

The crowd parted as she approached, their faces a mixture of relief and curiosity. Fairmont turned to face her, his smile tightening.

"Lady Ashcombe," he said smoothly. "How good of you to join us. I was just discussing the... challenges your new methods might bring."

"Challenges we are overcoming," Eva replied, her tone firm. "Ashcombe is thriving because of the trust and hard work of its people. The only obstacle we face is your interference."

A murmur of agreement rippled through the crowd, and Fairmont's expression darkened.

"You may have swayed the tenants," he said coldly, "but you cannot silence the truth."

Eva stepped closer, her gaze unwavering. "The truth is that Ashcombe's future will be decided by its people—not by a man who seeks only to control it. Your games won't work here, Fairmont. Not anymore."

The crowd erupted into applause, their support evident as Fairmont's composure faltered. He glared at Eva, his mask of civility slipping to reveal the bitterness beneath.

"This isn't over," he hissed before turning on his heel and striding away.

As the crowd began to disperse, their spirits visibly lifted, Nathaniel stepped beside Eva, his voice low. "You handled that brilliantly."

She exhaled slowly, the adrenaline beginning to fade. "I hope it's enough."

"It will be," Nathaniel said, his tone filled with quiet certainty. "Because you're showing them what true leadership looks like."

Eva glanced at him, her chest tightening with gratitude and something deeper. "Thank you," she said softly.

"Always," he replied, his gaze steady.

As they returned to the manor under the light of the moon, Eva felt a renewed sense of purpose. The challenges ahead would be difficult, but with Nathaniel by her side and the support of her community, she knew they could face anything.

Chapter Twenty-Nine

The village square was quiet the following morning, the only signs of the previous night's confrontation the trampled dirt and a lingering tension in the air. Despite the victory over Fairmont's attempted sabotage of her reputation, Eva knew the battle was far from over. His parting words echoed in her mind like a warning bell, and the specter of his influence loomed heavily over Ashcombe.

Back at the manor, Nathaniel found her in the drawing room, her shoulders tense as she read over reports from the tenants. The fire crackled softly in the hearth, its warmth doing little to ease the chill that had settled over her.

"You haven't stopped since we returned," Nathaniel said, his tone laced with gentle reproach.

Eva glanced up, offering a faint smile. "There's too much to do."

He crossed the room, leaning against the edge of the desk. "There always will be, Eva. But that doesn't mean you can't take a moment to breathe."

She sighed, setting the papers aside. "I just keep thinking about what he said. Fairmont won't give up, Nathaniel. He'll keep pushing until he finds a weakness to exploit."

"Then we won't give him one," Nathaniel replied firmly.

His certainty steadied her, and she nodded, her resolve strengthening. "You're right. He thrives on fear, and I won't give him the satisfaction of seeing us falter."

The next few days were a flurry of activity. Eva redoubled her efforts to strengthen ties with the tenants and tradesmen, visiting each family personally to address their concerns and reaffirm her commitment to their shared vision for Ashcombe.

Nathaniel organized patrols to ensure the estate's security, his leadership inspiring confidence among the workers. His ability to anticipate potential threats and defuse tension before it escalated proved invaluable, and Eva couldn't help but marvel at the quiet strength he brought to every situation.

One afternoon, as Eva returned from a meeting with a group of blacksmiths in the village, she found Sophia waiting for her in the foyer. Her sister's expression was unusually serious, and Eva felt a flicker of unease.

"What is it?" Eva asked, shrugging off her coat.

Sophia hesitated, her gaze darting to the door behind them before she spoke. "A letter arrived for you. From Fairmont."

Eva's stomach tightened, but she took the envelope from Sophia without hesitation. The seal was unmistakable, the heavy wax embossed with his family crest.

She broke the seal and unfolded the letter, her eyes scanning the carefully penned words. As she read, her unease deepened, the polite veneer of Fairmont's language failing to mask the thinly veiled threats woven throughout.

"He's not giving up," Eva said quietly, folding the letter and slipping it into her pocket.

Sophia frowned. "What does he want?"

"To remind me that he still believes Ashcombe should be his," Eva replied, her voice steady despite the anger simmering beneath the surface.

Sophia's expression hardened. "He's insufferable. What are you going to do?"

Eva squared her shoulders, her resolve firm. "I'm going to remind him that Ashcombe belongs to its people—not to him."

That evening, Eva sought out Nathaniel in the study, where he was reviewing the latest patrol reports. He looked up as she entered, his brow furrowing slightly at the tension in her expression.

"Another problem?" he asked.

"Fairmont," Eva replied, holding up the letter. "He's trying to intimidate me again. This time with threats cloaked in false courtesy."

Nathaniel's jaw tightened as he took the letter from her, his eyes scanning its contents. When he finished, he set it down with a quiet precision that belied the anger in his expression.

"He's testing your resolve," Nathaniel said, his voice low. "Trying to see if he can scare you into submission."

"Well, he can't," Eva said firmly. "But I won't let this escalate, either. The tenants have worked too hard to see their progress undone by his games."

Nathaniel nodded, his gaze steady. "Then we'll face him head-on. If he wants to push, we'll push back."

A faint smile tugged at Eva's lips. "You always make things seem so simple."

"It's not simple," Nathaniel said, his expression softening. "But it is clear. Ashcombe's future is worth fighting for—and so are you."

Her breath caught at the warmth in his voice, and she looked away, her cheeks flushing. "Thank you, Nathaniel. For standing with me. Always."

"Always," he echoed, his voice filled with quiet certainty.

The confrontation with Fairmont came sooner than Eva expected. Three days after the letter arrived, he appeared unannounced at the manor, his carriage rumbling into the courtyard with all the subtlety of a storm.

Eva met him in the drawing room, her posture poised and unyielding as he entered. Nathaniel stood just behind her, his presence a silent reminder of the strength that supported her.

"Lord Fairmont," Eva said coolly. "To what do we owe the pleasure?"

Fairmont's smile was thin, his eyes gleaming with calculated charm. "Lady Ashcombe. I thought it prudent to discuss the recent... disruptions on your estate."

Eva arched an eyebrow, her tone sharp. "Disruptions which, I suspect, you had a hand in."

Fairmont's smile didn't falter, but his gaze darkened. "I assure you, my intentions are purely honorable. I only wish to see Ashcombe prosper. And I fear your methods are putting that prosperity at risk."

Eva took a step forward, her voice unwavering. "The only risk to Ashcombe is you, Lord Fairmont. Your attempts to sow doubt and discord will not succeed. The tenants trust me, and they see the progress we're making. Your influence here is over."

Fairmont's expression hardened, his polished facade cracking under the weight of her defiance. "You're playing a dangerous game, Evangeline. You may have the tenants' favor now, but loyalty is fleeting. When things go wrong—and they will—you'll find yourself alone."

"She won't be alone," Nathaniel said, his voice calm but filled with steel.

Fairmont turned to him, his disdain evident. "Ah, Captain Grey. Ever the dutiful protector. But tell me—how long will your loyalty last when the odds turn against her?"

"As long as I live," Nathaniel replied without hesitation.

Fairmont's jaw tightened, but he said nothing more. Instead, he turned back to Eva, his voice low and icy. "You've made your position clear. But mark my words—this is far from over."

Eva held his gaze, her voice steady. "It is for you, Fairmont. Now, kindly see yourself out."

As the sound of Fairmont's carriage faded into the distance, Eva exhaled slowly, the tension draining from her shoulders.

Nathaniel stepped beside her, his expression softening. "You handled that brilliantly."

"Did I?" Eva asked, her voice tinged with weariness.

He nodded, his gaze filled with quiet pride. "You stood your ground. And you showed him that Ashcombe's strength comes from more than just you—it comes from everyone who believes in what you're building."

Her chest tightened at his words, and she turned to him, her voice trembling with emotion. "Thank you, Nathaniel. For being my strength when I need it most."

His lips curved into a faint smile, and he reached out, his hand brushing lightly against hers. "And you'll always have it."

As they stood together in the quiet drawing room, the fire casting flickering shadows around them, Eva felt a renewed sense of resolve. The fight for Ashcombe was far from over, but with Nathaniel by her side, she knew they could face whatever challenges lay ahead.

Chapter Thirty

The frost came early that year, blanketing the fields of Ashcombe in a silvery sheen that glistened under the pale light of the morning sun. The brisk air carried the promise of winter's approach, but the estate was alive with activity. The tenants worked tirelessly to bring in the last of the harvest, their faces flushed with cold and satisfaction as the barns filled with the fruits of their labor.

Eva stood at the edge of the field, her heart swelling with pride as she watched them. Despite Fairmont's meddling and the challenges they had faced, Ashcombe was thriving. The sight of the tenants working together—laughing, helping, and encouraging one another—was a testament to the strength of the community they had built.

Nathaniel approached from the far side of the field, his coat dusted with frost and his cheeks pink from the cold. He carried a ledger under one arm, his expression a mix of weariness and satisfaction.

"The final tallies are in," he said as he reached her. "It's better than we expected. Even with the damage to the eastern fields, we're on track for a surplus."

Eva let out a breath she hadn't realized she was holding, her relief evident. "That's wonderful news."

Nathaniel's lips curved into a faint smile. "It's more than wonderful, Eva. It's proof that what you've built here works."

She turned to him, her chest tightening with gratitude. "What we've built," she corrected gently.

His gaze softened, and for a moment, the cold seemed to melt away under the warmth of their connection.

Later that afternoon, Eva met with Mr. Cartwright in the estate office, the fire crackling softly in the hearth as they reviewed the accounts.

"The surplus gives us options, my lady," Cartwright said, his tone thoughtful. "We could reinvest in tools and infrastructure or set aside a portion for emergencies."

Eva tapped her fingers against the desk, considering the possibilities. "We should do both," she said finally. "The tenants have worked hard for this, and we need to ensure that their efforts are rewarded. But we also need to be prepared for whatever challenges lie ahead."

Cartwright nodded, his expression approving. "A wise decision, my lady. I'll see to it."

As he left the room, Eva leaned back in her chair, her mind already racing with plans for the coming months.

That evening, the manor was filled with a quiet sense of celebration. Sophia had insisted on organizing a small gathering for the tenants and workers, a chance to mark the end of the harvest and the beginning of a new chapter for Ashcombe.

The dining hall was warm and lively, the air filled with the sound of laughter and the clinking of glasses. Long tables were laden with hearty dishes, and the glow of candlelight reflected off the polished wood and gleaming silver.

Eva moved through the room, her presence met with smiles and words of gratitude from the tenants. She listened to their stories, laughed at their jokes, and offered quiet reassurances when worries surfaced.

"You've done something incredible here, Eva," Sophia said as she joined her near the head of the room.

Eva smiled, her heart swelling at her sister's words. "I didn't do it alone."

Sophia grinned, her gaze flicking toward Nathaniel, who was speaking with a group of tenants near the far wall. "No, you didn't."

As the evening wore on, Eva found herself stepping out onto the terrace to catch her breath. The cold air was a sharp contrast to the warmth of the hall, but it was invigorating, clearing her mind and calming her thoughts.

She wasn't alone for long.

Nathaniel joined her, his coat draped over his shoulders and his expression unreadable. He leaned against the stone railing beside her, the faint glow of the hall's light casting his features in sharp relief.

"Escaping the party?" he asked, his tone light.

"Just for a moment," Eva replied, her breath visible in the frosty air. "It's been... overwhelming, in the best possible way."

Nathaniel nodded, his gaze drifting toward the horizon. "You deserve it, Eva. You've worked harder than anyone to make this happen."

Her lips curved into a faint smile, and she turned to face him fully. "So have you."

He shook his head, his hazel eyes meeting hers. "This was always your vision. I just helped you find it."

Eva's chest tightened, her emotions threatening to spill over. "You've done so much more than that, Nathaniel. You've been my strength, my partner, my—"

She stopped herself, the words catching in her throat.

Nathaniel took a step closer, his voice soft but steady. "Your what?"

Her breath hitched, her heart pounding as she searched his gaze. "My everything," she whispered.

The words hung in the air between them, and then he closed the distance, his hands framing her face as his lips met hers. The kiss was soft but filled with an intensity that left her breathless, the warmth of his touch banishing the chill of the night.

When they parted, Nathaniel rested his forehead against hers, his voice barely above a whisper. "I love you, Eva."

Tears pricked at her eyes, and she smiled, her heart overflowing with joy and certainty. "I love you, too."

The rest of the evening passed in a blur of warmth and celebration, but as Eva lay in bed that night, her thoughts lingered on the moment she had shared with Nathaniel.

For the first time in years, the future felt bright, filled with possibility and hope.

And as she drifted off to sleep, her heart was light with the knowledge that she would never face it alone.

Chapter Thirty-One

The days after the harvest celebration were filled with a renewed sense of purpose across Ashcombe. The surplus had invigorated the tenants, and the repaired fences and fortified fields were a testament to their resilience. Yet, as winter's chill began to settle over the estate, Eva knew there would be no pause in the challenges they faced.

Fairmont might have retreated for the time being, but Eva doubted he would stay away for long. His ambitions for Ashcombe ran too deep, and his parting threats still lingered in her mind.

Eva found herself in the library one evening, a stack of correspondence spread out before her. Letters from Whitlock, neighboring landowners, and even the occasional inquiry from tradesmen filled her desk. The estate's growing reputation had drawn attention, much of it positive, but not all of it welcome.

Nathaniel entered quietly, his presence as grounding as ever. He carried two mugs of tea, setting one beside her before pulling up a chair.

"Long day?" he asked, his tone laced with gentle concern.

Eva sighed, her fingers brushing over the edge of one of the letters. "Long, but productive. Whitlock wants to expand our partnership again. He's suggesting we look into new irrigation systems for the fields."

Nathaniel nodded, his expression thoughtful. "That could be a game-changer. Especially with the unpredictable weather we've been seeing."

"It's ambitious," Eva said, her voice tinged with both excitement and apprehension. "But I think it's worth pursuing. The tenants deserve the best tools we can provide."

"They do," Nathaniel agreed. "And they trust you to make it happen."

Her lips curved into a faint smile, though her eyes remained on the papers before her. "Sometimes I wonder if I'm doing enough. If I'm making the right decisions."

Nathaniel reached out, his hand covering hers. "You are, Eva. And when you doubt yourself, remember that you don't have to do this alone. We're in this together."

Her heart swelled at his words, and she looked up, meeting his steady gaze. "Thank you," she said softly.

"Always," he replied, his voice filled with quiet conviction.

The next morning, Eva rose early, the pale light of dawn streaming through her windows as she dressed in warm layers. She had arranged to meet with a group of tenants in the eastern fields to discuss plans for the irrigation system, and she was eager to hear their thoughts.

As she stepped into the courtyard, she found Nathaniel waiting for her, his horse already saddled.

"You didn't think I'd let you go alone, did you?" he asked, a teasing smile playing at his lips.

Eva laughed softly, the sound light and unguarded. "I wouldn't dream of it."

They rode out together, the crisp air biting at their cheeks as the estate unfolded before them. The fields were quiet, the frost-tipped grass glistening under the soft light of the rising sun.

When they reached the eastern boundary, a group of tenants was already gathered, their faces alight with curiosity and cautious optimism. Eva dismounted, her boots crunching against the frozen ground as she approached them.

"Thank you all for coming," she said, her voice carrying across the quiet expanse of the fields. "I wanted to talk to you about the possibility of bringing in a new irrigation system. It's a significant investment, but one that could increase our yields and protect against droughts."

The tenants exchanged glances, their expressions thoughtful.

"It sounds promising," Mr. Harding said after a moment. "But how would it work? And what would it cost us?"

Eva nodded, her tone measured as she replied. "The cost would be shared between the estate and Lord Whitlock's partnership. As for how it works, we'd use trenches and pipes to ensure water is distributed evenly across the fields, even during dry spells."

Thomas, the younger tenant who had been vocal in earlier meetings, spoke up. "And what about the labor? Would we be expected to build it ourselves?"

Nathaniel stepped forward, his voice calm and reassuring. "We'll bring in experts to oversee the construction, but we'll need everyone's help to make it happen. This is an investment in the future—for all of us."

The tenants murmured among themselves, and Eva could sense their cautious acceptance.

"We'll think on it," Harding said finally. "But it sounds like it could be worth the effort."

"Thank you," Eva said, her smile genuine. "That's all I ask."

As they rode back to the manor, Eva felt a spark of hope igniting within her. The tenants' willingness to consider such a bold plan was a testament to the trust they had placed in her leadership.

"You handled that perfectly," Nathaniel said as they rode side by side.

Eva glanced at him, her cheeks flushed from the cold and his praise. "I just hope they see the potential in this. It could change everything for Ashcombe."

"They see it," Nathaniel replied. "Because you make them believe it's possible."

Her heart swelled at his words, and she turned her gaze back to the horizon, the future suddenly feeling brighter.

That evening, as the household gathered for supper, the mood was light. Sophia regaled them with stories from the village, her laughter infectious as she described the antics of the local children preparing for the winter festival.

Even Lady Margaret seemed more subdued, her sharp edges softened by the warmth of the family gathering.

"You've done well, Evangeline," Margaret said quietly as the meal drew to a close.

Eva looked up, surprised by the rare note of approval in her mother's voice. "Thank you, Mother."

Margaret's lips curved into a faint smile, and she inclined her head. "Ashcombe is thriving. And it's because of you."

The words lingered in Eva's mind long after the supper had ended, their weight both comforting and humbling.

Later that night, Eva found herself once again in the library, her thoughts turning to the future. The path ahead was still uncertain, but with each passing day, she felt more certain of her ability to navigate it.

Nathaniel joined her, his presence as steadying as ever.

"Still working?" he asked, his tone teasing.

"Always," Eva replied with a smile.

He chuckled, taking the seat across from her. "You never stop, do you?"

"I can't afford to," she said, her voice soft but determined. "Not when there's so much at stake."

Nathaniel's gaze softened, and he reached out, his hand brushing lightly against hers. "You've already accomplished so much, Eva. And I have no doubt you'll accomplish even more."

Her heart swelled at his words, and she smiled, her voice filled with quiet certainty. "Not without you."

"Then you'll never be without me," Nathaniel said, his voice low but firm.

As the fire crackled softly behind them, Eva felt a renewed sense of purpose settle over her. Together, they would face whatever challenges lay ahead—and together, they would ensure that Ashcombe's future remained bright.

Chapter Thirty-Two

Winter descended upon Ashcombe with an icy grip, the frost thickening into snow that blanketed the estate in soft, pristine white. The fields lay dormant under the weight of the season, their work completed for now, while the manor hummed with the quiet routines of preparation for the colder months.

Eva found herself drawn to the heart of these preparations. She moved between the manor and the village, ensuring that supplies were distributed fairly and that no tenant or worker was left wanting. The cold bit at her cheeks and fingers, but the gratitude in the villagers' eyes made every moment worthwhile.

One morning, as she finished overseeing the delivery of firewood to a family at the edge of the village, Eva spotted Nathaniel near the blacksmith's shop. He was deep in conversation with Mr. Cartwright, their breath visible in the icy air as they discussed the new patrol schedules.

She approached them, her boots crunching against the frozen ground. Nathaniel looked up as she neared, his smile breaking through the chill like a warm sunbeam.

"Everything all right?" he asked, his voice steady.

Eva nodded, her cheeks pink from the cold. "The families are well-stocked for now, but we'll need to arrange another delivery before the next snowstorm."

Cartwright tipped his hat to her, his expression approving. "You've done good work, my lady. The tenants appreciate it more than you know."

"Thank you, Mr. Cartwright," Eva said warmly.

As the steward excused himself to tend to other matters, Nathaniel turned to her, his gaze thoughtful. "You've been out here for hours. Have you even eaten today?"

Eva laughed softly, brushing a strand of hair from her face. "I'll eat when I'm finished."

Nathaniel arched an eyebrow, his tone turning teasing. "Stubborn as ever, I see."

She smiled, her heart lifting at his familiar humor. "I prefer to think of it as determined."

"Of course," he replied, his lips curving into a faint smile. "Then let me be equally determined in making sure you get something warm to eat. Come on."

They returned to the manor, the warmth of the great hall a welcome contrast to the biting cold outside. Sophia met them near the hearth, her cheeks flushed as she arranged fresh garlands of evergreen and holly along the mantel.

"You're just in time," Sophia said brightly, her eyes sparkling with mischief. "Cook has been working on a stew that could revive even the iciest of souls."

Eva laughed, shedding her cloak and gloves. "That sounds perfect."

As they sat down at the long oak table, the aroma of the hearty stew filled the air, and Eva felt a wave of contentment settle over her. The familiar clatter of utensils and the warmth of Sophia's chatter made the manor feel more like a home than it had in years.

That evening, as the snow fell softly outside, Eva and Nathaniel found themselves in the library once again. The fire crackled in the hearth, its light casting flickering shadows across the walls lined with books.

Nathaniel was seated at the desk, reviewing reports from the patrols, while Eva sat in the armchair by the fire, a blanket draped over her lap and a cup of tea warming her hands.

"You've been quiet tonight," Nathaniel said, glancing up from his work.

Eva smiled faintly, her gaze fixed on the flames. "Just thinking."

"About?" he prompted gently.

She hesitated, her fingers tightening around the teacup. "About everything. The estate, the tenants, the future."

Nathaniel set the reports aside, crossing the room to sit in the chair opposite hers. "What about the future worries you?"

Eva met his gaze, her voice soft but steady. "Everything feels so fragile, Nathaniel. Even with the progress we've made, it could all fall apart if we're not careful."

He leaned forward, his elbows resting on his knees. "That's true of anything worth building. But you're not alone in this, Eva. The tenants believe in you, Whitlock supports you, and..." He hesitated, his voice softening. "And I'll always be here, no matter what."

Her chest tightened at his words, and she set the teacup aside, her fingers brushing lightly against his. "I know. And I can't tell you how much that means to me."

Nathaniel's gaze softened, and he reached out, his hand closing over hers. "Then let me say it again—I'm here. Always."

The weight of his sincerity settled over her like a warm blanket, and she smiled, her heart swelling with gratitude and something deeper.

The next morning brought fresh challenges. Reports from the northern edge of the estate indicated that several trees had been brought down by the snow, blocking access to a small cluster of tenant cottages.

Eva and Nathaniel rode out together, their horses trudging through the thick drifts as they made their way to the affected area. The scene was worse than expected—large oaks had fallen across the path, their branches intertwined in a tangled, icy mass.

"It'll take days to clear this," Nathaniel said, dismounting to inspect the damage.

Eva frowned, her mind racing. "The tenants in those cottages can't wait that long. We'll need to organize a team to clear the path immediately."

Nathaniel nodded, his tone decisive. "I'll gather the workers and bring the tools. You can coordinate supplies for the tenants—they'll need extra firewood and food until this is cleared."

They worked side by side throughout the day, the cold biting at their hands and faces as they directed the effort. By nightfall, the path was partially cleared, enough to allow access to the cottages and deliver the much-needed supplies.

As they returned to the manor, exhausted but satisfied, Eva turned to Nathaniel, her voice soft. "Thank you for today. I couldn't have managed without you."

He smiled, his gaze steady. "You didn't need me, Eva. But I'm glad I was here."

Her heart swelled at his words, and she smiled, the cold forgotten in the warmth of his presence.

That night, as the snow continued to fall outside, Eva stood by her bedroom window, gazing out at the white-covered landscape. Despite the challenges they had faced that day, she felt a quiet sense of contentment.

Ashcombe was thriving, and with Nathaniel by her side, the future felt less daunting and more hopeful.

And for the first time in years, she allowed herself to dream—not just of a prosperous estate, but of a life filled with love, partnership, and the enduring strength of a community bound by trust.

Would you like me to continue with Chapter Thirty-Three? It will delve into the deepening stakes for Ashcombe and explore the growing relationship between Eva and Nathaniel.

As the days grew shorter and December settled over Ashcombe, the estate began to hum with preparations for Christmas. The tenants brought fresh greenery from the woods, decking the great hall with garlands of pine and holly. Sophia took charge of the decorations, her laughter echoing through the manor as she enlisted every available hand to hang wreaths and trim the towering Christmas tree that had been brought in from the forest.

On Christmas Eve, the manor glowed with warmth and light. Candles flickered in every window, their soft glow reflected in the polished wood and garlands of greenery that adorned the rooms. The great hall had been transformed into a haven of festive cheer, its long tables laden with an array of dishes that filled the air with the mouthwatering scent of roasted meats, spiced cider, and sweet puddings.

Eva stood near the hearth, her hands clasped in front of her as she watched the tenants and workers gather around the tree. Laughter and music filled the room, the strains of a fiddle mingling with the soft hum of conversation.

"You've created something beautiful," Nathaniel said, stepping beside her.

Eva turned to him, her cheeks pink from the warmth of the fire and the praise in his voice. "We've created it," she replied softly.

His lips curved into a faint smile, and for a moment, they stood in comfortable silence, watching as the children darted around the tree, their laughter bright and unguarded.

As the evening wore on, the crowd began to thin, families returning to their cottages with full bellies and warm hearts. By the time the last guests departed, only a handful of people remained in the great hall. Sophia was seated near the hearth, chatting animatedly with Mr. Cartwright, while Eva and Nathaniel lingered near the tree, its ornaments catching the light of the fire.

Nathaniel reached up, adjusting a star at the top of the tree. "It's a bit crooked," he said, his tone teasing.

Eva laughed, shaking her head. "It's perfect, Nathaniel. Just like tonight."

He turned to her, his gaze softening. "It is, isn't it?"

Eva nodded, her voice quiet. "For the first time in years, it feels like Ashcombe is truly alive again."

Nathaniel stepped closer, his voice low and steady. "That's because of you, Eva. You brought this place back to life."

Her chest tightened at his words, and she looked away, her cheeks flushing. "I couldn't have done it without you."

He reached out, his fingers brushing lightly against hers. "Maybe not. But it's your heart, your determination, that's made all of this possible."

Their eyes met, and for a moment, the world seemed to still, the warmth of his presence filling the quiet space between them.

"I have something for you," Nathaniel said suddenly, breaking the silence.

Eva blinked, startled. "You do?"

He smiled faintly, reaching into his coat pocket and pulling out a small box wrapped in simple brown paper.

"I wasn't sure when to give it to you," he admitted, his tone almost shy.

Eva took the box, her heart pounding as she carefully unwrapped it. Inside was a delicate silver locket, its surface etched with intricate floral patterns.

"Nathaniel," she whispered, her voice trembling.

"It reminded me of you," he said softly. "Strong, beautiful, and full of life."

Tears pricked at her eyes, and she looked up at him, her voice barely above a whisper. "It's perfect. Thank you."

He reached out, taking the locket from her and fastening it around her neck. His fingers brushed lightly against her skin, sending a shiver down her spine.

When he stepped back, his gaze lingered on her, his voice filled with quiet intensity. "Merry Christmas, Eva."

She smiled, her heart swelling with emotion. "Merry Christmas, Nathaniel."

The warmth of that moment stayed with Eva as she lay in bed that night, the locket resting against her chest like a silent promise. For the first time in years, Christmas felt not only joyful but full of hope, a testament to the strength of the bonds they had forged and the love that had blossomed amid the challenges they faced.

As snow fell softly outside, blanketing Ashcombe in a peaceful hush, Eva drifted to sleep, her heart light with the knowledge that she was exactly where she was meant to be.

Chapter Thirty-Three

The new year dawned with a crisp clarity that seemed to promise a fresh beginning for Ashcombe. The snow that blanketed the fields sparkled under the winter sun, and the tenants returned to their tasks with renewed energy, bolstered by the successes of the previous months.

Eva felt a sense of optimism she hadn't known in years. The Christmas celebration had brought the estate together in a way that felt deeply meaningful, and the quiet moments she had shared with Nathaniel lingered in her heart, warming her even as the frost persisted.

On the first day of January, Eva called a meeting of the tenants and workers in the great hall. She stood before them with Nathaniel at her side, her hands clasped in front of her as she addressed the crowd.

"Last year was one of change and challenge," she began, her voice steady and clear. "But it was also a year of growth and progress. Together, we've accomplished more than I ever imagined possible, and Ashcombe is stronger because of each and every one of you."

A murmur of agreement rippled through the crowd, and Eva felt a swell of pride.

"As we move into this new year, I want to share with you the plans we have for Ashcombe," she continued. "With the surplus from last year's harvest, we'll be investing in new tools and infrastructure, as well as an irrigation system that will ensure our fields thrive no matter what the weather brings."

The announcement was met with murmurs of excitement, and Eva glanced at Nathaniel, drawing strength from his quiet presence.

"We'll need your help to make this vision a reality," she said, her gaze sweeping over the gathered faces. "But I have no doubt that, together, we can continue to build a future we can all be proud of."

The applause that followed was genuine and heartfelt, and Eva felt a deep sense of gratitude for the trust and support of the community.

As the meeting concluded and the tenants began to disperse, Nathaniel turned to Eva, his expression filled with quiet pride.

"You've inspired them, Eva," he said softly.

"They inspire me," she replied, her voice trembling with emotion.

The weeks that followed were filled with activity as plans for the irrigation system took shape. Eva worked tirelessly with Mr. Cartwright and Lord Whitlock's advisors, reviewing designs and overseeing the procurement of materials. Nathaniel, as always, was at the center of the effort, organizing the workers and ensuring that every detail was accounted for.

The project was ambitious, but Eva was determined to see it through. The tenants had placed their trust in her, and she was resolved to honor that trust by giving them the tools they needed to succeed.

One cold, clear afternoon, Eva and Nathaniel rode out to the fields to inspect the progress on the initial trenches for the irrigation system. The workers moved with quiet efficiency, their breath visible in the frosty air as they dug through the frozen ground.

"This will change everything for them," Eva said, her voice filled with quiet wonder as she surveyed the work.

Nathaniel nodded, his expression thoughtful. "It's a testament to what's possible when people believe in something bigger than themselves."

She turned to him, her gaze softening. "And when they have someone like you to guide them."

He smiled faintly, his hazel eyes warm. "They don't need me, Eva. They have you."

Her heart swelled at his words, and she looked away, her cheeks flushed. "We're a team, Nathaniel. I couldn't do this without you."

"Nor I without you," he replied, his tone quiet but certain.

As the days lengthened and the snow began to melt, the progress on the irrigation system became a source of pride for the entire community. The once-dormant fields began to show the first signs of life, and the tenants' excitement was palpable.

One evening, as the sun dipped below the horizon, casting the estate in hues of gold and lavender, Eva stood at the edge of the fields with Nathaniel, their breath visible in the cool air.

"It's happening," she said softly, her voice filled with awe.

"It is," Nathaniel replied, his gaze steady. "Because you never gave up."

She turned to him, her eyes shining. "Because we never gave up."

He smiled, his expression filled with quiet affection. "Together, Eva. Always."

As the first stars appeared in the night sky, Eva felt a profound sense of hope for the future. Ashcombe was thriving, and the bonds they had forged—between the tenants, the workers, and each other—were stronger than ever.

And as she stood there, hand in hand with Nathaniel, she knew that the best was yet to come.

Chapter Thirty-Four

The promise of spring began to creep into the air, melting the last of the snow and filling Ashcombe with the first hints of new life. The fields, dark and rich with thawed earth, were ready to be sown, and the tenants worked with renewed vigor as the irrigation system neared completion.

Eva moved through the days with a quiet sense of satisfaction, her heart lighter than it had been in years. The estate was thriving, the tenants were flourishing, and she had never felt more connected to the place she called home—or to the people who had helped her rebuild it.

On a bright morning in late February, Eva stood at the edge of the eastern fields, watching as the first test of the irrigation system began. Water coursed through the carefully dug trenches, spreading evenly across the soil in a steady, controlled flow.

The tenants gathered around, their faces alight with awe and excitement as the system proved its worth.

"It's working!" Thomas exclaimed, his voice filled with amazement.

"It's better than working," Mr. Harding added, his tone gruff but approving. "This will change everything for us."

Eva smiled, her chest swelling with pride. "It's because of all of you," she said, her voice steady. "This is the result of your hard work and trust. Together, we've created something extraordinary."

The applause that followed was spontaneous and heartfelt, and Eva felt a wave of gratitude wash over her.

Nathaniel stepped beside her, his gaze fixed on the flowing water. "It's a remarkable thing, isn't it?" he said softly.

She turned to him, her voice filled with quiet emotion. "It's more than remarkable. It's a beginning."

The success of the irrigation system was celebrated with a feast at the manor, the great hall once again filled with laughter and warmth. Sophia had outdone herself, organizing an array of dishes that showcased the best of Ashcombe's resources.

As the tenants and workers gathered around the long tables, Eva stood at the head of the room, raising a glass to address them.

"To Ashcombe," she said, her voice carrying across the room. "To the strength of this community and the future we're building together."

The cheers that followed were jubilant, and Eva felt a surge of hope for what lay ahead.

Later that evening, as the celebration began to wind down, Eva found herself walking through the quiet halls of the manor. The moonlight streamed through the tall windows, casting a soft glow over the polished floors.

She stepped into the library, the fire in the hearth burning low, and found Nathaniel there, seated in one of the armchairs with a glass of brandy in hand.

"I thought I might find you here," she said, her tone light as she crossed the room.

He looked up, a faint smile tugging at his lips. "And I thought you'd still be in the hall, basking in your well-earned triumph."

Eva laughed softly, sinking into the chair opposite him. "It's not just my triumph. It's ours."

Nathaniel studied her for a moment, his hazel eyes thoughtful. "You've done something extraordinary, Eva. You've given these people hope—and a future they can believe in."

Her heart swelled at his words, and she looked away, her cheeks flushing. "I couldn't have done it without you."

He leaned forward slightly, his voice quiet but firm. "You could have. But I'm glad you didn't have to."

Their eyes met, and for a moment, the room seemed to still, the weight of their connection filling the space between them.

"Nathaniel," Eva began, her voice trembling, "I don't think I've ever thanked you properly—for everything."

He reached out, his hand brushing lightly against hers. "You don't need to thank me, Eva. Being here, with you—it's more than enough."

Her breath caught at the sincerity in his voice, and she smiled, her chest tightening with emotion. "I don't know what the future holds, but I know I want you to be part of it."

"I'm not going anywhere," Nathaniel said, his tone steady. "Wherever you go, I'll be there."

As the fire crackled softly behind them, Eva felt a quiet sense of certainty settle over her. The challenges ahead might be daunting, but with Nathaniel by her side, she knew they could face anything.

In the weeks that followed, the first seeds were planted in the newly irrigated fields, their rows straight and even under the watchful eyes of the tenants. The sense of hope that had taken root during the winter began to blossom, and Ashcombe buzzed with the promise of a bountiful spring.

For Eva, the days were long and filled with work, but they were also filled with joy. The bonds she had forged—with the tenants, with her family, and with Nathaniel—gave her a strength she hadn't known she possessed.

And as the first green shoots began to peek through the soil, Eva felt a deep, abiding sense of gratitude for the journey that had brought her to this moment.

Ashcombe was thriving, and so was she.

Chapter Thirty-Five

Spring arrived at Ashcombe with an explosion of life. The fields were awash in shades of green, the crops thriving under the careful watch of the tenants and the nourishment of the irrigation system. The air was filled with the scent of fresh blooms, and the estate buzzed with a quiet energy that seemed to reflect the optimism of its people.

Eva moved through her days with a renewed sense of purpose. The hard work of the past year was bearing fruit, and the community she had worked so tirelessly to rebuild was flourishing. But with the estate's success came new challenges, and Eva was determined to meet them head-on.

One morning, as the sunlight filtered through the tall windows of the manor's dining room, Sophia burst in with a letter clutched in her hand.

"This just arrived," Sophia said breathlessly, waving the envelope. "It's from Lord Whitlock."

Eva set down her teacup, her curiosity piqued. "What does he say?"

Sophia handed her the letter, her eyes sparkling with excitement. "He wants to host a gathering at his estate—a chance for neighboring landowners to see what we've accomplished with the partnership."

Eva's chest tightened with a mix of excitement and apprehension as she read the letter. "It's an incredible opportunity," she said slowly. "But it's also a chance for scrutiny."

"Which you'll handle brilliantly," Sophia said with unwavering confidence. "This is your moment, Eva. Whitlock wouldn't invite you if he didn't believe in what you've built."

Eva nodded, her resolve hardening. "Then we'll prepare. This is a chance to secure Ashcombe's future—and I won't let it slip away."

The days leading up to the gathering were a whirlwind of preparation. Eva worked closely with Nathaniel and Mr. Cartwright to assemble reports, maps, and visual aids that would showcase Ashcombe's progress.

Sophia, ever the social strategist, coached Eva on how to navigate the gathering with poise and confidence.

"Remember," Sophia said as she adjusted the collar of Eva's dress on the morning of the event, "you've already proven yourself. This is just about showing them what they already know—you're a force to be reckoned with."

Eva smiled faintly, her nerves tempered by her sister's encouragement. "Thank you, Sophia. For everything."

Sophia grinned, stepping back to admire her handiwork. "You're going to dazzle them, Eva. Now, go show them what Ashcombe is made of."

The journey to Whitlock Manor was bathed in the soft light of a spring morning. The trees lining the road were heavy with blossoms, their petals falling like snow as Eva and Nathaniel rode side by side.

"You seem calm," Nathaniel observed, his tone light.

Eva glanced at him, her lips curving into a faint smile. "I feel ready," she admitted. "For the first time, I'm not questioning whether I belong in that room."

"You've always belonged," Nathaniel said, his hazel eyes steady. "They're just starting to realize it."

His words sent a warm rush through her chest, and she felt a renewed sense of confidence as Whitlock Manor came into view.

The gathering was held in Whitlock's grand ballroom, its high ceilings and arched windows flooding the space with natural light. Landowners from across the region mingled, their conversations a mix of curiosity and admiration as they discussed the success of the Ashcombe-Whitlock partnership.

Eva moved through the crowd with Nathaniel at her side, her posture poised and her gaze steady as she answered questions and shared insights. The visual aids she had prepared were met with enthusiasm, and more than one landowner expressed interest in adopting similar methods on their own estates.

Whitlock himself approached midway through the gathering, his expression warm and approving.

"Lady Ashcombe," he said, extending a hand. "You've surpassed every expectation. The work you've done is nothing short of transformative."

"Thank you, Lord Whitlock," Eva replied, her voice steady. "But I couldn't have done it without your support—or the dedication of Ashcombe's people."

He smiled, his gaze flicking to Nathaniel. "And, I suspect, the guidance of a certain captain."

Nathaniel inclined his head, his tone respectful. "It's been an honor to be part of this effort, my lord."

Whitlock chuckled, his eyes twinkling. "A partnership in every sense of the word, then. Ashcombe is lucky to have you both."

As he moved on to greet another guest, Eva turned to Nathaniel, her chest tightening with gratitude.

"You've always believed in me," she said softly. "Even when I wasn't sure I could do this."

Nathaniel's gaze softened, and he reached out, his hand brushing lightly against hers. "That's because I've always seen what you're capable of, Eva. And I always will."

The gathering was a resounding success, and as Eva and Nathaniel rode back to Ashcombe that evening, the setting sun painted the sky in hues of pink and gold.

"You were remarkable today," Nathaniel said as they approached the manor.

Eva smiled, her heart light with the triumph of the day. "So were you. I couldn't have done it without you."

"You'll never have to," he replied, his voice steady.

As they passed through the gates of Ashcombe, Eva felt a profound sense of accomplishment. The partnership had not only secured the estate's future but had also cemented her place as a leader in the community.

And with Nathaniel by her side, she knew that whatever challenges lay ahead, they would face them together.

Chapter Thirty-Six

The weeks following the gathering at Whitlock Manor were filled with a renewed sense of purpose across Ashcombe. The event had solidified the estate's reputation as a model of innovation and resilience, and the interest expressed by other landowners hinted at future opportunities that could secure its prosperity for years to come.

For Eva, the success of the gathering was both validating and energizing. Yet, even as she immersed herself in the work of managing the estate and expanding its reach, a quiet awareness lingered in the back of her mind—an awareness of the deepening connection between her and Nathaniel.

One breezy afternoon, Eva stood on the veranda overlooking the southern fields. The wind carried the scent of freshly turned earth and the faint hum of tenants working in the distance. She had just finished reviewing a letter from Lord Whitlock proposing an expansion of their resource-sharing agreement when Nathaniel appeared at her side.

"Busy as ever," he said, his tone teasing as he gestured toward the papers in her hand.

Eva smiled, tucking the letter into her pocket. "You wouldn't expect anything less, would you?"

"Not at all," he replied with a grin. "But even you deserve a break now and then."

She raised an eyebrow, her tone light. "And what exactly do you propose, Captain Grey?"

Nathaniel nodded toward the stables. "A ride. Just the two of us. The estate is thriving, the tenants are happy, and you've earned at least an hour to enjoy it."

Eva hesitated, the weight of her responsibilities tugging at her. But the warmth in Nathaniel's gaze made her relent.

"All right," she said with a laugh. "Lead the way."

The ride took them along the estate's western boundary, where the fields gave way to rolling hills and patches of wildflowers. The air was fresh and crisp, the first signs of summer beginning to emerge in the vibrant greens of the landscape.

As they rode side by side, Eva felt a sense of freedom she hadn't known in months. The rhythm of the horses' hooves and the gentle sway of the countryside seemed to strip away the pressures of her position, leaving only the simple pleasure of the moment.

They reached a hill overlooking the estate and dismounted, the view stretching out before them like a painting. The manor stood at the heart of the land, its stone walls gleaming in the sunlight, surrounded by fields that teemed with life.

"It's beautiful," Eva said softly, her gaze sweeping over the scene.

Nathaniel stood beside her, his hands resting lightly on his hips. "It is. But it's more than that—it's alive. Because of you."

Her chest tightened, and she turned to him, her voice trembling. "Because of us."

Nathaniel's lips curved into a faint smile, his hazel eyes warm. "I'm just the one who makes sure the fences stay up and the tenants don't get into too much trouble. You're the one who brought this place back to life."

Eva shook her head, her heart swelling with emotion. "You've done so much more than that, Nathaniel. You've been my strength, my partner... my friend."

He stepped closer, his voice low and steady. "And I'll be all of those things for as long as you'll have me."

Her breath hitched, and she reached out, her hand brushing lightly against his. "Then I hope you'll be here forever."

Nathaniel's smile widened, and he reached up to cup her cheek, his touch warm and grounding. "Forever, Eva. Always."

As their lips met in a soft, lingering kiss, the world seemed to fall away, leaving only the quiet certainty of their love.

The ride back to the manor was filled with a comfortable silence, the air between them charged with unspoken promises. When they reached the stables, the late afternoon sun cast long shadows over the courtyard, and Eva felt a sense of peace settle over her.

Sophia met them as they dismounted, her expression alight with curiosity. "You two look suspiciously cheerful," she said, her tone teasing.

Eva laughed, shaking her head. "Just enjoying the estate."

Sophia's gaze flicked between them, her grin widening. "If you say so."

That evening, as Eva sat in the library reviewing the latest tenant reports, Nathaniel entered with a sheaf of papers in hand.

"Cartwright finished the breakdown of last month's expenditures," he said, setting the papers on the desk.

"Thank you," Eva replied, her tone warm.

Nathaniel lingered, his gaze steady. "You seemed happy today. More at ease."

Eva looked up, her lips curving into a soft smile. "I am. For the first time in a long time, I feel like I'm exactly where I'm meant to be."

Nathaniel's expression softened, and he reached out, his hand brushing lightly against hers. "Then let's keep building on it. Together."

"Together," Eva echoed, her heart swelling with gratitude and hope.

As the days turned into weeks, the partnership between Eva and Nathaniel deepened, their shared vision for Ashcombe weaving their lives together in ways neither had anticipated.

The estate continued to thrive, but for Eva, the true measure of success was the quiet certainty she felt in her heart—the knowledge that she was not only building a future for Ashcombe but also for herself, with the man who had become her anchor, her partner, and her love.

Chapter Thirty-Seven

The warmth of summer seeped into Ashcombe, transforming the fields into seas of green and gold. The irrigation system had exceeded expectations, and the tenants worked with a confidence born of success, their efforts reflected in the thriving crops and bustling activity throughout the estate.

For Eva, the long days were filled with both satisfaction and a constant hum of anticipation. The future of Ashcombe seemed brighter than ever, but she knew from experience that progress was never without its challenges.

One afternoon, as the sun blazed high in the sky, Eva was in the manor's office reviewing reports from the tenants. A knock at the door drew her attention, and Nathaniel entered, his shirt sleeves rolled up and his hair slightly tousled from the summer heat.

"Cartwright asked me to bring these," he said, setting a stack of papers on the desk.

"Thank you," Eva replied, her lips curving into a smile.

Nathaniel lingered, his gaze thoughtful. "You've been at this all day. When's the last time you stepped outside?"

Eva laughed softly, shaking her head. "I lose track of time when there's so much to do."

He arched an eyebrow, his tone teasing. "Then it's my duty to remind you that there's an entire estate out there waiting to be admired. Come on, take a break."

She hesitated, her responsibilities tugging at her. But the warmth in Nathaniel's gaze made her relent.

"All right," she said, rising from her chair. "Where are you taking me?"

"You'll see," he replied with a grin.

Nathaniel led her to a shaded grove at the edge of the estate, where the trees provided a welcome respite from the heat. A small stream ran through the clearing, its gentle babble adding to the tranquility of the setting.

Eva gasped softly as she noticed a picnic spread out on the grass, complete with a basket of fresh bread, cheese, and fruit.

"You did this?" she asked, her voice filled with surprise.

Nathaniel shrugged, his expression sheepish. "You've been working too hard. I thought you deserved a moment to enjoy yourself."

Her heart swelled at the gesture, and she smiled, her voice soft. "Thank you, Nathaniel. This is... perfect."

They sat together under the shade of a large oak tree, the soft rustle of leaves and the stream's steady flow creating a peaceful backdrop.

For a while, they simply enjoyed the moment, sharing stories and laughter as they ate. But as the conversation slowed, Nathaniel's expression grew more serious.

"Do you ever think about what's next?" he asked, his voice quiet.

Eva tilted her head, studying him. "For Ashcombe?"

"For you," he clarified, his gaze steady.

She hesitated, her thoughts swirling. "Ashcombe is my life, Nathaniel. I've spent so long fighting for this place—I'm not sure I know how to think beyond it."

He nodded, his lips curving into a faint smile. "It's a part of who you are. But it's not all of who you are."

Eva's breath caught at the weight of his words, and she looked away, her cheeks flushing. "What about you? Do you think about the future?"

Nathaniel's expression softened, and he reached out, his hand brushing lightly against hers. "I think about it all the time. And the only thing I know for certain is that I want you to be part of it."

Her heart swelled, and she turned back to him, her voice trembling. "I want that, too."

As the sunlight filtered through the leaves, casting dappled patterns over them, Eva felt a quiet certainty settle in her chest. For the first time, the future didn't feel like a daunting unknown—it felt like a promise.

That evening, as they returned to the manor, Eva's thoughts lingered on the moments they had shared. The quiet intimacy of their connection and the unspoken possibilities that lay ahead filled her with both excitement and a sense of peace.

Sophia was waiting for them in the courtyard, her hands on her hips and her expression playfully exasperated.

"Running off without telling me? Honestly, Eva, I thought we were past secrets," she teased.

Eva laughed, shaking her head. "It wasn't a secret. Just a much-needed escape."

Sophia's gaze flicked between them, her grin widening. "Well, whatever it was, it seems to have done you good. You're glowing."

Eva's cheeks flushed, but she didn't deny it.

As the days turned into weeks, the bond between Eva and Nathaniel grew stronger, their partnership extending beyond the work of the estate into the quiet moments they shared.

The challenges of the past seemed to fade into the background, replaced by the steady progress of Ashcombe and the quiet certainty of their love.

And as the first hints of autumn began to creep into the air, Eva felt a sense of anticipation building within her—a sense that the best was yet to come.

Chapter Thirty-Eight

As summer gave way to autumn, Ashcombe flourished in ways Eva had only dreamed of a year ago. The tenants worked with a renewed sense of pride, their fields yielding a harvest that exceeded all expectations. The irrigation system had proven its worth, and the once-precarious estate now stood as a model of innovation and resilience.

For Eva, the season marked not just the culmination of months of hard work but also the beginning of something deeper—both within herself and in her bond with Nathaniel.

One crisp September morning, Eva was in the fields alongside the tenants, her skirts gathered as she helped gather bushels of wheat. The air was filled with the hum of conversation and the rhythmic sound of scythes cutting through stalks.

Nathaniel arrived on horseback, his presence commanding but unassuming. The tenants greeted him warmly, their trust in him evident in their easy smiles and nods of respect.

"Busy morning?" he asked as he dismounted, approaching Eva with a faint grin.

Eva brushed a strand of hair from her face, her cheeks pink from the exertion. "Every morning is busy, Nathaniel. You should know that by now."

He chuckled, his hazel eyes crinkling at the corners. "Fair enough. I thought I'd lend a hand."

"Lending a hand?" Thomas called out from a few rows away. "More like trying to outshine the rest of us."

The tenants laughed, and Nathaniel held up his hands in mock surrender. "I wouldn't dream of it."

Eva smiled, her heart light as she watched the easy camaraderie between Nathaniel and the workers. His presence had become as much a part of Ashcombe as the land itself, and she couldn't imagine the estate—or her life—without him.

By late afternoon, the work was done, and the fields were quiet, the golden light of the setting sun casting long shadows over the land. Eva and Nathaniel walked side by side along the edge of the fields, their steps slow and unhurried.

"The tenants seem happy," Nathaniel said, his tone thoughtful.

"They are," Eva replied, her gaze sweeping over the horizon. "Ashcombe is thriving because of their hard work and belief in this place. It's everything I hoped for—and more."

Nathaniel glanced at her, his expression soft. "And you, Eva? Are you happy?"

She hesitated, the question settling over her like a warm blanket. "I think... I'm learning how to be. For so long, my focus was on saving Ashcombe. But now, I'm starting to see that there's more to life than just this land."

Nathaniel stopped, turning to face her. "There is. And you deserve to experience all of it."

Her breath caught at the intensity in his gaze, and she looked away, her voice trembling. "I don't know if I'd even know where to begin."

He reached out, his hand brushing lightly against hers. "You begin by letting yourself dream, Eva. And when you're ready, I'll be there to help make those dreams a reality."

Her chest tightened, and she looked up at him, her heart swelling with gratitude and something deeper. "Nathaniel, you've already given me so much. I don't know how I could ever—"

"You don't have to," he interrupted gently. "Just let me stand by you. That's all I've ever wanted."

Tears pricked at her eyes, and she nodded, her voice barely above a whisper. "Always."

That evening, the manor was alive with the sounds of laughter and music as the tenants gathered to celebrate the harvest. Long tables were set up in the courtyard, laden with hearty dishes and jugs of cider.

Sophia, ever the life of the party, flitted from table to table, her infectious energy drawing smiles and laughter from everyone she encountered.

Eva sat beside Nathaniel at the head of the main table, her heart light as she watched the people of Ashcombe revel in the fruits of their labor.

"This," she said softly, gesturing to the scene before them, "is everything I hoped for."

Nathaniel reached for her hand under the table, his grip warm and steady. "It's just the beginning, Eva."

She turned to him, her chest tightening at the quiet certainty in his voice. "I believe you."

As the celebration wound down and the last of the tenants departed for their cottages, Eva and Nathaniel lingered in the courtyard. The air was cool and still, the stars twinkling above them like scattered diamonds.

"I have something for you," Nathaniel said, breaking the comfortable silence.

Eva raised an eyebrow, her curiosity piqued. "Oh?"

He reached into his coat and pulled out a small wooden box, its surface polished and smooth. "It's nothing grand," he said, his tone almost shy. "But I saw it and thought of you."

Eva opened the box, her breath catching as she revealed a delicate silver bracelet, its links adorned with tiny charms—a rose, a wheat sheaf, a star. Each one a symbol of Ashcombe and the journey they had shared.

"Nathaniel," she whispered, her voice trembling.

"It's a reminder," he said softly. "Of everything you've built. Of everything you are."

Tears filled her eyes as she slipped the bracelet onto her wrist, the cool metal warming against her skin. "It's perfect. Thank you."

He reached out, brushing a tear from her cheek. "You're perfect, Eva."

As their lips met in a soft, lingering kiss, Eva felt the weight of the past year melt away, leaving only the quiet certainty of their love and the promise of a future filled with hope and possibility.

Chapter Thirty-Nine

The days of early autumn stretched on, golden and unhurried, as Ashcombe settled into a rhythm of prosperity. The harvest had been a success, the tenants were thriving, and the manor bustled with activity.

For Eva, these days felt like a gift. She had fought so hard to bring Ashcombe to life, and now, for the first time, she could truly savor what they had built. The land that once bore the weight of uncertainty now thrived with hope, and her heart felt lighter with each passing day.

One crisp morning, Eva stood at the edge of the orchard, watching as workers gathered apples for cider pressing. The air was filled with the sweet scent of ripe fruit, and the soft rustling of leaves provided a soothing backdrop.

Nathaniel approached from the path leading to the stables, his coat dusted with hay and his hair ruffled by the wind.

"Admiring your kingdom?" he teased, his tone warm.

Eva laughed softly, turning to face him. "It's not a kingdom, Nathaniel. It's a community. And it's because of everyone's hard work, not just mine."

He arched an eyebrow, his lips curving into a faint smile. "Modest as always."

She shook her head, her gaze drifting back to the orchard. "It's true. None of this would have been possible without the tenants, the workers—and you."

Nathaniel's expression softened, and he stepped closer, his voice low. "I've been thinking about something."

Eva glanced at him, her curiosity piqued. "What is it?"

He hesitated for a moment, then gestured to the land around them. "This place—it's more than just an estate. It's a home. A future. And I've realized that I don't want to be anywhere else."

Her breath caught, the weight of his words settling over her like a warm blanket. "Nathaniel..."

He reached out, his hand brushing lightly against hers. "I love you, Eva. And I want to spend my life here, with you."

Tears pricked at her eyes, and she smiled, her voice trembling. "I love you too, Nathaniel. More than I ever thought possible."

The days that followed were filled with quiet joy as Eva and Nathaniel settled into their new understanding. Their partnership, already unshakable, deepened in ways that felt both comforting and exhilarating.

Together, they continued to guide Ashcombe through its transformation, their shared vision for the estate bringing them closer with each passing day.

One evening, as the sun dipped below the horizon, casting the manor in hues of amber and rose, Sophia burst into the library, her expression alight with excitement.

"You'll never guess what I've just heard!" she exclaimed, waving a letter in her hand.

Eva looked up from her seat by the fire, raising an eyebrow. "Something tells me you're going to tell me anyway."

Sophia grinned, plopping into the chair opposite her. "Lord Whitlock has invited us to a ball at his manor next month. It's to celebrate the success of the partnership and the progress we've made here."

Eva's lips curved into a faint smile. "That's wonderful news. It will be a good opportunity to show the other landowners that Ashcombe's success is more than just a fleeting moment."

"It will also be a good opportunity for you to wear something other than those practical dresses you insist on," Sophia teased, her eyes twinkling.

Eva laughed, shaking her head. "I'll consider it."

The weeks leading up to the ball were filled with anticipation. Sophia took charge of arranging their travel and wardrobes, her excitement infectious as she planned every detail.

Eva, meanwhile, worked tirelessly to ensure that the estate would run smoothly in her absence. Though the idea of leaving Ashcombe, even for a few days, filled her with unease, she trusted Nathaniel and the tenants to manage in her stead.

"I think you're more worried about this than you were about Fairmont," Nathaniel teased one evening as they reviewed the estate's accounts.

Eva smiled, her cheeks flushing. "Ashcombe has been my whole world for so long. It's hard to step away, even for something as important as this."

Nathaniel reached out, his hand covering hers. "You've built something strong, Eva. Strong enough to stand without you for a few days. And if anything goes wrong, I'll be here to handle it."

Her heart swelled at his words, and she nodded, her voice soft. "Thank you, Nathaniel. For always being here."

"Always," he replied, his gaze steady.

When the day of the ball arrived, the journey to Whitlock Manor was filled with a mix of excitement and nerves. Sophia chattered animatedly as their carriage rolled through the countryside, her enthusiasm making Eva laugh despite her own apprehension.

"You look stunning," Sophia said as they approached the manor, her gaze lingering on Eva's gown—a soft, flowing creation in a shade of deep blue that brought out the warmth in her eyes.

"Thank you," Eva replied, her cheeks pink.

As they entered the grand ballroom, the sight before them took Eva's breath away. The room was a masterpiece of opulence, its high ceilings adorned with glittering chandeliers and its floors polished to a mirror-like shine.

Eva moved through the crowd with quiet poise, Nathaniel at her side, his presence grounding her as they navigated the sea of unfamiliar faces.

The evening was a triumph, with Lord Whitlock himself praising Ashcombe's achievements and introducing Eva to influential figures who expressed admiration for her leadership.

By the time the ball concluded, Eva felt both exhilarated and exhausted, the weight of the evening's success settling over her like a warm embrace.

As they returned to Ashcombe under the light of a full moon, Eva leaned back in her seat, her gaze drifting to Nathaniel.

"You were incredible tonight," he said softly, his voice filled with pride.

She smiled, her heart light. "So were you."

He reached for her hand, his grip warm and steady. "We make a good team, don't we?"

Eva nodded, her voice filled with quiet certainty. "The best."

As the carriage rolled on through the night, Eva felt a profound sense of gratitude for the journey that had brought her here—to Ashcombe, to Nathaniel, and to a future filled with hope and love.

Chapter Forty

The success of the ball at Whitlock Manor rippled through the region like a warm breeze, carrying with it whispers of Ashcombe's resurgence. Eva returned to the estate with a renewed sense of purpose, her heart buoyed by the validation of her efforts and the quiet strength of Nathaniel's unwavering support.

As the days passed, letters arrived in a steady stream—notes of congratulations, requests for advice, and even tentative inquiries about potential collaborations. Ashcombe was no longer a struggling estate on the brink of ruin; it was a beacon of possibility, and Eva found herself at the heart of it all.

One morning, as Eva sat at her desk in the manor's study, reviewing a particularly intriguing proposal from a neighboring landowner, Sophia burst in, her expression alight with excitement.

"You'll want to see this," Sophia said, holding up an envelope sealed with a distinctive crest.

Eva raised an eyebrow, setting her papers aside. "What is it?"

"An invitation," Sophia replied, handing her the letter. "From Lord Ashbury himself."

Eva's breath caught as she broke the seal, the weight of the invitation sinking in as she read its contents. Lord Ashbury was one of the most influential figures in the region, and his estate was known for its grand gatherings of landowners and visionaries.

"He's invited us to a summit," Eva said, her voice tinged with wonder. "To discuss the future of agriculture and land stewardship."

Sophia grinned, her eyes sparkling. "This is huge, Eva. If Ashcombe is represented there, it will solidify everything you've worked for."

Eva nodded, her thoughts racing. The opportunity was undeniable, but it also came with immense pressure.

"Will you go?" Sophia asked, her tone eager.

Eva hesitated for only a moment before meeting her sister's gaze. "Yes. Ashcombe deserves a seat at that table."

Preparations for the summit began immediately, with Eva and Nathaniel working tirelessly to assemble data and reports that showcased Ashcombe's innovations and success.

"You're going to impress them," Nathaniel said one evening as they pored over maps and ledgers in the library.

Eva smiled faintly, her fingers tracing the lines of a carefully drawn chart. "I hope so. This could open doors I never thought possible."

"It will," Nathaniel replied, his tone steady. "Because you've earned it."

Her chest tightened at his words, and she glanced at him, her voice soft. "I couldn't have done any of this without you."

His gaze softened, and he reached out, his hand brushing lightly against hers. "You would have found a way, Eva. But I'm glad I've been here to help."

The day of the summit dawned clear and bright, the crisp air filled with the scent of autumn leaves. Eva dressed carefully, her gown a muted green that echoed the colors of the land she represented.

Nathaniel accompanied her, his steady presence a source of comfort as they traveled to Lord Ashbury's estate.

The summit was held in a sprawling hall adorned with rich tapestries and banners that represented the gathered estates. The air buzzed with conversation, the hum of anticipation mingling with the clink of glasses and the rustle of papers.

Eva moved through the crowd with quiet confidence, her head held high as she introduced herself to landowners and dignitaries. Nathaniel was never far from her side, his calm demeanor and thoughtful contributions adding weight to her presence.

When it was her turn to speak, Eva stood before the assembly, her heart pounding as she surveyed the room.

"Ladies and gentlemen," she began, her voice steady despite the nerves that fluttered in her chest. "I am honored to stand before you as a representative of Ashcombe. Our journey has been one of challenge and transformation, and I am here to share the lessons we've learned along the way."

She spoke of the irrigation system, the tenants' resilience, and the importance of collaboration between landowners and workers. Her words were met with murmurs of approval and nods of agreement, and as she finished, the applause that followed was genuine and heartfelt.

Later, as the summit drew to a close, Eva found herself standing on the terrace, gazing out over the rolling hills that surrounded Ashbury's estate.

Nathaniel joined her, his expression thoughtful. "You were remarkable today," he said softly.

Eva smiled, her cheeks flushing. "It was a team effort."

He reached out, his hand brushing against hers. "It was your vision, Eva. And now, everyone else can see what I've always known—you're a force to be reckoned with."

Her heart swelled at his words, and she turned to him, her voice trembling. "Thank you, Nathaniel. For believing in me."

"Always," he replied, his gaze steady.

As they returned to Ashcombe under the light of a waning moon, Eva felt a deep sense of gratitude for the journey that had brought her to this moment. The future stretched out before her, vast and filled with possibility, and she knew that, whatever challenges lay ahead, she would face them with Nathaniel by her side.

Ashcombe was no longer just an estate—it was a legacy, a testament to the strength of community and the power of love and determination. And for Eva, it was home.

Chapter Forty-One

The days following the summit brought a new sense of momentum to Ashcombe. The praise and interest Eva had garnered during her presentation led to a steady stream of letters from neighboring landowners and potential collaborators, each eager to learn from Ashcombe's success.

But with this newfound recognition came challenges. The attention placed Ashcombe under greater scrutiny, and Eva knew she would have to navigate these waters carefully to ensure that the estate's growth remained sustainable and grounded in the principles she held dear.

One crisp morning, as the first frost of the season clung to the ground, Eva sat in the study, a fresh stack of correspondence spread out before her. Nathaniel entered quietly, a cup of tea in each hand.

"Thought you could use this," he said, setting one down beside her.

Eva smiled, her fingers brushing lightly against his as she accepted the cup. "You always know what I need."

He chuckled, his hazel eyes warm. "You've been working nonstop since we returned. What's the latest?"

She gestured to the letters. "More proposals. Some of them are intriguing, but others..." She sighed, shaking her head. "It's clear that not everyone understands what we're trying to build here."

Nathaniel leaned against the edge of the desk, his tone thoughtful. "That's because what you're doing is different, Eva. It's not just about profits or prestige—it's about people. And that's not something everyone knows how to value."

His words settled over her like a warm blanket, and she nodded, her resolve strengthening. "Then I'll keep showing them. Ashcombe's success isn't just ours—it's something that can inspire others to think differently."

"And you'll do it brilliantly," Nathaniel said, his voice filled with quiet certainty.

Her heart swelled at his unwavering support, and she reached out, her hand brushing lightly against his. "Thank you, Nathaniel. For always believing in me."

"Always," he replied, his gaze steady.

Later that day, Eva met with Mr. Cartwright in the estate office to discuss the logistics of expanding Ashcombe's resources to meet the growing demand for its methods.

"We'll need to be cautious, my lady," Cartwright said, his tone measured. "While the interest is promising, overextending ourselves could put us at risk."

Eva nodded, her expression thoughtful. "Agreed. Let's prioritize partnerships with those who align with our values. We've worked too hard to build this foundation to compromise it now."

Cartwright's lips curved into a faint smile. "A wise decision, as always."

As autumn deepened, the estate buzzed with activity. The tenants worked to prepare the fields for winter, their efforts a testament to the strong community that had taken root at Ashcombe.

Eva spent her days immersed in the work of the estate, but her evenings were increasingly filled with quiet moments shared with Nathaniel. Their bond had grown stronger with each passing day, and though neither had spoken explicitly of the future, it was clear in the way they moved through the world together that their lives were deeply intertwined.

One evening, as the first hints of winter crept into the air, Eva and Nathaniel walked through the gardens, their breath visible in the chilly twilight.

"The tenants seem optimistic," Nathaniel said, his tone warm.

"They are," Eva replied, her gaze sweeping over the darkened fields. "And so am I. For the first time in years, it feels like we're not just surviving—we're thriving."

Nathaniel glanced at her, his expression thoughtful. "That's because of you, Eva. You've given them something to believe in."

Her cheeks flushed at his praise, and she looked away, her voice soft. "I couldn't have done it alone."

"You didn't have to," he replied gently. "But you're the one who led us here."

Her chest tightened at the weight of his words, and she turned to face him, her heart pounding. "Nathaniel, I don't know what the future holds. But I know I want you to be part of it."

He reached out, his hand cupping her cheek as his gaze met hers. "You have me, Eva. Now and always."

As their lips met in a soft, lingering kiss, Eva felt a quiet certainty settle over her. The path ahead might be filled with challenges, but with Nathaniel by her side, she knew they could face anything.

The weeks that followed were filled with preparation as Ashcombe transitioned into the winter season. The tenants worked tirelessly to secure the estate, their efforts a testament to the strength of the community they had built together.

For Eva, these days were a reminder of how far they had come—and how much more was possible.

And as the first snowflakes began to fall, dusting Ashcombe in a blanket of white, Eva felt a profound sense of gratitude for the journey that had brought her to this moment.

Ashcombe was more than just a home; it was a legacy, a testament to the power of resilience, hope, and love.

And for Eva, it was the beginning of a future filled with promise and possibility.

Chapter Forty-Two

Winter settled over Ashcombe like a soft blanket, the snow transforming the fields into a serene expanse of white. The crisp air carried the scent of pine and wood smoke, and the manor glowed with warmth as fires burned steadily in its many hearths.

For Eva, the season marked a time of reflection and planning. The flurry of attention following the summit had eased, giving her space to refocus on the heart of Ashcombe—the people who had made its transformation possible.

One morning, as the first light of dawn filtered through the frosted windows of the dining room, Eva sat at the long oak table, reviewing the estate's winter accounts. The fire crackled softly in the hearth, and the steaming cup of tea beside her added a touch of comfort to the quiet moment.

Nathaniel entered, his boots muffled against the thick rugs as he carried a stack of papers under one arm.

"Good morning," he said, his voice warm as he set the papers down in front of her.

"Good morning," Eva replied, looking up with a smile. "What's this?"

"Updates from the tenants," he explained, pulling out a chair beside her. "Cartwright thought you'd want to see them."

Eva picked up the top sheet, scanning its contents. Her smile widened as she read the notes of gratitude and progress from the workers.

"They're thriving," she said softly, her heart swelling. "Even in winter, they're finding ways to keep moving forward."

"That's because of you," Nathaniel said, his gaze steady.

Her cheeks flushed, and she shook her head. "It's because of all of us. This is their victory as much as mine."

Nathaniel leaned back in his chair, a faint smile playing at his lips. "You'll never take the credit, will you?"

Eva laughed, the sound light. "Not when there's so much to share."

As the day unfolded, Eva found herself drawn to the gardens, where the snow-covered hedges and frosted branches created a landscape of quiet beauty. She pulled her cloak tighter against the chill as she walked, her breath visible in the crisp air.

Nathaniel joined her there, his presence as steady and grounding as ever.

"Enjoying the snow?" he asked, his tone teasing.

"It's beautiful," Eva replied, her gaze sweeping over the glistening landscape. "Peaceful."

He nodded, his hazel eyes thoughtful. "A moment to breathe before the next challenge."

She glanced at him, her lips curving into a faint smile. "You're always ready for what's next, aren't you?"

"It's part of the job," he said with a grin. "But even I know how to appreciate the quiet moments."

They walked in companionable silence for a while, the only sound the crunch of their boots against the snow.

"Do you ever think about what's next?" Eva asked suddenly, her voice soft.

Nathaniel tilted his head, his expression thoughtful. "I think about it all the time. But lately, my thoughts keep coming back to one thing—or rather, one person."

Eva's breath caught, her heart pounding as she turned to him.

"I've spent my life looking for purpose, Eva," Nathaniel continued, his voice low. "And I've found it here—with you. I can't imagine a future that doesn't include you."

Her chest tightened, and she reached out, her fingers brushing lightly against his. "I feel the same. You've been my anchor, Nathaniel. My partner. My everything."

His gaze softened, and he stepped closer, his voice trembling with emotion. "Then let me be that for you—always."

Eva's breath hitched, and she nodded, her voice barely above a whisper. "Always."

That evening, the manor was alive with warmth and laughter as the tenants and workers gathered for a midwinter celebration. The great hall was filled with the scent of roasted meats and spiced cider, and the air buzzed with the hum of conversation and the occasional burst of laughter.

Sophia had taken charge of the decorations, adorning the hall with garlands of evergreen and twinkling candles.

"Eva, you have to try the cider," Sophia said, appearing at her side with a cup in hand. "It's the best batch yet."

Eva laughed, accepting the cup and taking a sip. The warmth of the spiced drink spread through her, and she smiled. "It's wonderful."

"Just like tonight," Sophia said, her gaze sweeping over the bustling hall. "You've created something incredible, Eva. Ashcombe is thriving—and so are you."

Eva's cheeks flushed, and she glanced across the room to where Nathaniel stood, talking with Mr. Cartwright. His easy smile and the quiet strength in his demeanor filled her with a sense of peace she hadn't known in years.

"Maybe I am," she said softly, her heart full.

As the celebration wound down and the guests began to depart, Eva found herself standing on the terrace, gazing out over the snow-covered fields. The moonlight bathed the landscape in a silvery glow, and the air was still and quiet.

Nathaniel joined her, his presence warm against the chill of the night.

"Beautiful, isn't it?" he said, his voice low.

Eva nodded, her gaze fixed on the horizon. "It feels... timeless. Like everything we've worked for is finally settling into place."

"It is," Nathaniel said, turning to face her. "Because of you."

She looked up at him, her heart swelling with emotion. "Because of us."

He reached out, his hand brushing lightly against her cheek. "Eva, I—"

Before he could finish, she leaned up, her lips meeting his in a soft, lingering kiss.

When they parted, her voice was a whisper against the night. "I love you, Nathaniel."

His eyes shone with quiet intensity. "And I love you. More than I ever thought possible."

As they stood together under the light of the moon, Eva felt a quiet certainty settle over her. The future was theirs to build, and with Nathaniel by her side, she knew it would be filled with hope, love, and endless possibility.

Chapter Forty-Three

The cold of winter deepened over Ashcombe, but within the manor and its community, a warmth persisted—a resilience that Eva had come to treasure. The estate, once teetering on the brink of ruin, now thrived not only in its fields and finances but in the hearts of its people.

As the days inched closer to spring, Eva found herself balancing the demands of leadership with the unexpected joy of a deepening bond with Nathaniel. Their relationship had become a quiet anchor in her life, a steady source of strength that carried her through even the most trying moments.

One morning, Eva stood in the library, a map of the estate spread out before her. Nathaniel entered, carrying a steaming cup of tea.

"You're spoiling me," Eva said with a smile as she accepted the cup.

"I like to think of it as practical support," Nathaniel replied, his tone teasing.

She chuckled, taking a sip of the tea before gesturing to the map. "I was thinking about the northern fields. They've been underutilized for years, but with the success of the irrigation system, I believe we can make them productive again."

Nathaniel leaned over the map, his brow furrowing as he studied the area she indicated. "You're right. The soil there is good—it just needs the right attention. And if we rotate the crops strategically, we can avoid overworking the land."

Eva nodded, her excitement building. "Exactly. It'll take time, but the potential is worth the effort."

Nathaniel glanced at her, his hazel eyes warm. "It's a good plan, Eva. And with the tenants behind you, I have no doubt it'll succeed."

Her chest tightened at the quiet confidence in his voice, and she reached out, her hand brushing lightly against his. "Thank you, Nathaniel. For always seeing the possibilities."

"Because you make them clear," he replied, his voice soft.

Later that day, as Eva walked through the village, she was greeted with smiles and nods from the tenants. The bonds she had forged with them were stronger than ever, and their gratitude for her leadership was evident in every interaction.

She stopped to speak with Thomas, who was repairing a fence near the southern cottages.

"My lady," Thomas said, tipping his hat. "Word's spread about your plans for the northern fields. The tenants are eager to get started."

Eva smiled, her heart swelling with pride. "I'm glad to hear it. With everyone's efforts, I'm confident we can make it a success."

Thomas nodded, his expression thoughtful. "You've given us more than just a livelihood, my lady. You've given us hope."

The sincerity in his voice brought a lump to Eva's throat, and she nodded, her voice steady. "It's because of all of you that Ashcombe is what it is today. I'm just grateful to be part of it."

That evening, as the manor settled into a quiet rhythm, Eva found herself in the drawing room with Nathaniel. The fire crackled softly in the hearth, casting flickering shadows across the walls.

Nathaniel was seated in one of the armchairs, a glass of brandy in hand. Eva sat across from him, a book resting on her lap.

For a while, they simply enjoyed the silence, the warmth of the fire and each other's presence filling the room with an unspoken intimacy.

"What are you thinking about?" Nathaniel asked suddenly, his voice breaking the quiet.

Eva looked up, her lips curving into a faint smile. "About the future. About everything we've accomplished—and everything that's still to come."

He leaned forward slightly, his gaze steady. "And how does it look?"

Her smile widened, a quiet certainty settling over her. "Bright. Full of possibility."

Nathaniel's expression softened, and he reached out, his fingers brushing lightly against hers. "It's because of you, Eva. You've built something extraordinary here."

She shook her head, her voice filled with emotion. "Because of us, Nathaniel. I couldn't have done it without you."

"You won't have to," he replied, his voice low but firm.

As their hands intertwined, Eva felt a profound sense of gratitude for the journey that had brought her to this moment. The challenges they had faced, the victories they had won—all of it had led to a future she could truly believe in.

As winter began to wane and the first hints of spring crept into the air, Eva and Nathaniel worked side by side to prepare Ashcombe for the season ahead. The northern fields, long neglected, were plowed and sown with care, their potential finally being realized.

For Eva, the work was more than just a task—it was a testament to the strength of the community they had built and the love that had taken root in her heart.

And as the days grew longer and the fields began to show the first signs of life, she knew that the best was yet to come.

Chapter Forty-Four

Spring arrived at Ashcombe with an energy that seemed to ripple through every corner of the estate. The fields, dark and rich with newly turned soil, were alive with activity as tenants planted the first crops of the season. The northern fields, which had been dormant for so long, now showed rows of green shoots peeking through the earth, a testament to the hard work and vision that had brought them back to life.

For Eva, the season felt like a new beginning. The challenges of the past seemed distant now, replaced by the quiet satisfaction of seeing Ashcombe thrive. And at the center of it all was Nathaniel, whose presence had become as steady and vital to her as the land itself.

One morning, Eva stood on the veranda, the warm breeze carrying the scent of fresh blossoms and damp earth. The sky was a brilliant blue, and the hum of activity from the fields below added to the sense of promise that filled the air.

Nathaniel joined her, his boots tapping softly against the wooden planks as he approached.

"It's a good day," he said, his voice filled with quiet satisfaction.

"It is," Eva agreed, her gaze sweeping over the estate. "Everything feels... hopeful."

Nathaniel leaned against the railing, his hazel eyes thoughtful. "It's more than hope, Eva. It's progress. Everything you've worked for is coming to life."

Her chest tightened at the warmth in his words, and she turned to him, her voice soft. "Everything we've worked for."

His lips curved into a faint smile, and he reached out, his hand brushing lightly against hers. "Together, then."

"Always," she replied, her heart swelling with gratitude and love.

As the day unfolded, Eva and Nathaniel moved through the estate, their focus on preparing for the upcoming planting festival—a tradition that had long been dormant at Ashcombe but one that Eva had decided to revive.

"It's a chance to bring everyone together," Eva explained as they walked through the village. "To celebrate the land and the people who make this place what it is."

Nathaniel nodded, his expression approving. "The tenants will love it. And it's another way to show them how much you value their efforts."

"I hope so," Eva said, her voice tinged with anticipation. "I want it to be more than just a celebration—I want it to be a promise. That Ashcombe's future is something we'll all share."

The days leading up to the festival were filled with preparation. The tenants decorated the village square with garlands of flowers and ribbons, while the workers set up long tables for the feast. Sophia threw herself into the planning with her usual enthusiasm, overseeing everything from the menu to the music.

"This will be the best festival Ashcombe has ever seen," Sophia declared one afternoon, her cheeks flushed with excitement. "Just wait and see."

Eva laughed, her sister's energy infectious. "I have no doubt it will be."

The festival day dawned clear and bright, the kind of spring morning that seemed to carry the promise of endless possibility. The village square buzzed with activity as families gathered, their laughter and chatter filling the air.

Eva stood at the heart of it all, her heart swelling as she watched the community come together. Nathaniel was never far from her side, his presence steadying as they moved through the crowd, greeting tenants and sharing in their excitement.

As the feast began, Eva raised her glass, her voice carrying over the gathered crowd.

"To Ashcombe," she said, her tone filled with emotion. "To the land that sustains us and the people who make it thrive. This festival is a celebration of all that we've accomplished together—and a promise of the future we'll continue to build."

The cheers that followed were loud and heartfelt, and Eva felt a wave of gratitude wash over her.

Later, as the sun dipped below the horizon, casting the village in hues of gold and amber, Eva and Nathaniel stood at the edge of the square, watching as children danced and families lingered by the firelight.

"It's perfect," Nathaniel said, his voice soft.

Eva glanced at him, her lips curving into a smile. "It is."

He turned to her, his gaze steady. "You've done something remarkable here, Eva. You've built more than just an estate—you've built a home. For everyone."

Her chest tightened at his words, and she reached out, her hand brushing lightly against his. "Because of you, Nathaniel. I couldn't have done this without you."

His smile widened, and he took her hand in his, his grip warm and reassuring. "And you'll never have to."

As they stood together, the firelight flickering around them and the sounds of the festival filling the air, Eva felt a quiet certainty settle over her.

Ashcombe was thriving, her heart was full, and the future stretched out before her like an endless horizon. And for the first time, she felt truly at peace.

Chapter Forty-Five

The planting festival lingered in the hearts of Ashcombe's tenants and workers long after the last ribbons were taken down and the final songs were sung. Its success marked a turning point—not just for the estate, but for the spirit of its people. A sense of unity, rare and deeply cherished, had taken root alongside the crops that now thrived in the fields.

For Eva, the festival's success was both a triumph and a reminder of the delicate balance she sought to maintain. With Ashcombe's reputation growing beyond its borders, the demands on her time and attention were greater than ever. And while she relished the challenges, she also longed for moments of quiet with the people who had become her foundation—especially Nathaniel.

The weeks following the festival were filled with plans for the northern fields. The tenants had thrown themselves into the project with enthusiasm, but the sheer scale of the endeavor required careful coordination.

One sunny morning, Eva found herself standing at the edge of the northern fields, her boots sinking into the soft earth as she studied the rows of sprouting plants. Nathaniel rode up on horseback, his coat dusted with dirt and his hair tousled by the wind.

"I've just spoken with Harding," he said, dismounting smoothly. "He's concerned about the schedule for the irrigation channels. If the rains come late, we'll need to adjust."

Eva nodded, her brow furrowing as she considered the implications. "Then we'll prioritize this section first," she said, gesturing to the easternmost row. "It's the most vulnerable to dry spells."

Nathaniel stepped beside her, his gaze following hers. "It's a good call. Harding trusts your judgment, you know."

A faint smile touched her lips. "He didn't always."

"Maybe not," Nathaniel said with a grin. "But you've earned it—and more."

His words sent a warmth through her chest, and she glanced at him, her voice soft. "You make it sound so simple."

"It is," he replied, his gaze steady. "Because you're doing it for the right reasons."

Eva looked away, her cheeks flushing under the weight of his praise. "Thank you, Nathaniel. For always seeing what I sometimes can't."

The days passed in a flurry of activity as the northern fields took shape. Eva worked alongside the tenants, her hands as busy as her mind. She dug trenches, adjusted plans, and listened to the workers' concerns, her presence a constant reassurance.

Nathaniel was never far away, his quiet strength and practical wisdom invaluable as they navigated the challenges of the project.

One afternoon, as they paused to eat a quick lunch under the shade of a tree, Nathaniel leaned back against the trunk, his expression thoughtful.

"You've been restless lately," he said, his tone gentle.

Eva looked up from her bread and cheese, her brow furrowing. "Restless?"

He nodded, his hazel eyes searching hers. "You've been pushing yourself harder than ever. It's like you're trying to prove something—to yourself, maybe."

Her chest tightened at his words, and she looked away, her voice barely above a whisper. "Sometimes I wonder if it's enough. If I'm enough."

Nathaniel straightened, his voice firm but kind. "Eva, look around you. These fields, these people—none of this would be possible without you. You've built something extraordinary, not because you're trying to prove anything, but because you care."

Her throat tightened, and she met his gaze, her voice trembling. "I don't want to fail them, Nathaniel. Or you."

"You won't," he said simply, his gaze steady. "Because you're not alone. You have them, and you have me."

Tears pricked at her eyes, and she nodded, her voice barely above a whisper. "Thank you."

"Always," he replied, his hand brushing lightly against hers.

As spring deepened into early summer, the northern fields began to flourish, their rows of crops standing tall and vibrant under the warm sun. The tenants' pride in their work was evident in their smiles and the easy camaraderie that filled the air.

For Eva, the fields were more than just a success—they were a symbol of what Ashcombe could become.

One evening, as the sun dipped below the horizon, casting the estate in hues of gold and pink, Eva stood on the hill overlooking the fields. Nathaniel joined her, his presence as steadying as ever.

"It's beautiful, isn't it?" she said softly, her voice filled with wonder.

"It is," Nathaniel agreed, his gaze on her rather than the fields. "But it's nothing compared to what you've created here."

Her cheeks flushed, and she looked away, her voice trembling. "It's not just me, Nathaniel. It's us."

He stepped closer, his voice low and steady. "Eva, I've been thinking about the future—our future."

Her breath caught, and she turned to face him, her heart pounding.

"I've spent my life searching for a place to belong," Nathaniel continued, his hazel eyes filled with quiet intensity. "And I've found it here, with you. I want to build that future together—here, at Ashcombe."

Tears filled her eyes, and she nodded, her voice trembling. "I want that too. More than anything."

As he took her hand in his, the warmth of his touch grounding her, Eva felt a quiet certainty settle over her.

The future stretched out before them, vast and filled with possibility. And for the first time, she felt truly at peace.

Chapter Forty-Six

The days following Cartwright's revelation were a whirlwind of preparation. Eva worked tirelessly to gather records, maps, and tenant testimonies that would prove Ashcombe's irrigation project was not only ethical but beneficial to the region.

Nathaniel stood at the heart of the effort, his presence a steadying force as he coordinated with Cartwright and advised Eva on how to approach the council. Despite the looming threat, he never wavered in his confidence.

"You've faced worse, Eva," he reminded her one evening as they pored over documents in the study. "And you've always come out stronger."

"I've never had so much to lose," Eva admitted softly, her voice trembling with the weight of her fears.

Nathaniel reached across the table, his hand closing over hers. "And you've never had so much to fight for. That's what will make the difference."

The hearing was set for a week later, to be held in the council hall of the neighboring town. The tenants rallied around Eva, their loyalty and determination unwavering. They knew the stakes as well as she did, and their support only strengthened her resolve.

On the morning of the hearing, the manor was alive with activity as tenants loaded wagons with bundles of evidence and supplies for the journey. Sophia flitted between the workers, her usual levity tempered by a quiet determination.

"You've got this," Sophia said as Eva adjusted her traveling cloak. "And if Fairmont thinks he can outsmart you, he's in for a rude awakening."

Eva smiled faintly, grateful for her sister's unshakable belief in her. "Thank you, Sophia. For always being in my corner."

"Always," Sophia replied, her grin widening. "Now, go show them what Ashcombe is made of."

The journey to the council hall was tense but uneventful. Eva and Nathaniel rode at the head of the procession, their expressions resolute despite the weight of what lay ahead.

When they arrived, the hall was already bustling with landowners, council members, and curious onlookers. Fairmont stood near the front, his polished veneer hiding the malice that simmered beneath.

"Lady Ashcombe," he said smoothly as she approached. "How good of you to join us. I trust you've come prepared to answer for your... overreach."

Eva met his gaze without flinching. "Ashcombe's success speaks for itself, Lord Fairmont. But I'm more than happy to present the truth."

Fairmont's smile tightened, and he inclined his head. "We'll see."

The hearing began with Fairmont presenting his case, his words laced with half-truths and veiled accusations. He painted Ashcombe's irrigation system as a reckless endeavor that had disrupted neighboring estates and caused unnecessary hardship.

When it was Eva's turn to speak, she rose with quiet confidence, her heart pounding but her voice steady.

"Ladies and gentlemen of the council," she began, her gaze sweeping the room. "Ashcombe was once a struggling estate, on the brink of collapse. Its revival is not the result of recklessness, but of innovation, determination, and the shared efforts of its people."

She presented maps and records that detailed the careful planning and execution of the irrigation system, highlighting its benefits not just to Ashcombe but to the surrounding region.

"Far from causing harm," Eva continued, her voice ringing with conviction, "Ashcombe's methods have served as a model of what is possible when we work with the land, rather than against it. The success of our tenants is proof of what can be achieved through collaboration and foresight."

The murmurs that rippled through the room were ones of approval, and Eva felt a flicker of hope.

When the council called for testimonies, several of Ashcombe's tenants stepped forward to speak on Eva's behalf. Their words were simple but powerful, painting a picture of a community that had been transformed under her leadership.

"I've lived on Ashcombe land my whole life," Harding said, his voice steady. "And I've never seen it thrive the way it does now. That's because of Lady Ashcombe and the choices she's made—not for herself, but for all of us."

The council members exchanged glances, their expressions thoughtful.

As the hearing concluded, Eva stood outside the hall with Nathaniel, her nerves taut as they awaited the council's decision.

"You were brilliant," Nathaniel said, his voice filled with quiet pride.

Eva glanced at him, her lips curving into a faint smile. "I hope it was enough."

"It was," he replied firmly.

When the council members emerged, their verdict was clear: the petition was denied. Ashcombe's methods were found to be both ethical and exemplary, and the council commended Eva for her leadership.

Relief washed over her as the crowd dispersed, and she turned to Nathaniel, her chest tight with emotion.

"We did it," she said softly.

"No," he replied, his gaze steady. "You did it."

The journey back to Ashcombe was filled with quiet celebration, the tension of the past weeks finally giving way to a sense of triumph.

When they arrived at the manor, the tenants greeted them with cheers and applause, their joy infectious as they celebrated the victory.

That evening, as the estate settled into the quiet rhythms of night, Eva and Nathaniel stood together on the terrace, the moonlight casting a silver glow over the fields.

"This isn't just a victory for Ashcombe," Eva said, her voice filled with quiet wonder. "It's a promise of what's to come."

Nathaniel reached for her hand, his grip warm and steady. "The future is yours, Eva. And I'll be with you every step of the way."

Her heart swelled at his words, and she turned to him, her voice trembling. "Ours, Nathaniel. The future is ours."

As their lips met in a soft, lingering kiss, Eva felt a quiet certainty settle over her. The challenges they had faced were only the beginning, and the future stretched out before them—vast, bright, and filled with possibility.

Chapter Forty-Seven

The victory over Fairmont's petition had solidified Ashcombe's standing as a model of innovation and resilience. The tenants and workers, emboldened by the affirmation of their efforts, tackled the spring planting season with vigor, the estate humming with activity from sunrise to sunset.

For Eva, the days were long but deeply fulfilling. Her vision for Ashcombe had taken root in ways she hadn't dared to dream, and the unity she felt with the people and the land filled her with quiet pride. Yet, even as the estate flourished, Eva couldn't shake the sense that new challenges loomed on the horizon.

One evening, Eva sat at her desk in the study, the warm glow of the fire casting flickering shadows on the walls. She was poring over a letter from Lord Whitlock, his elegant script detailing an ambitious proposal to expand their partnership.

Nathaniel entered, his coat slung over one arm and his boots leaving faint traces of dirt on the rug.

"You're still at it," he said, his tone affectionate as he crossed the room to stand beside her.

Eva looked up, her lips curving into a faint smile. "There's always more to do."

"What's caught your attention this time?" Nathaniel asked, leaning over her shoulder to glance at the letter.

"Whitlock wants to collaborate on a project to build shared storage facilities for surplus crops," Eva explained. "It's a bold idea, but it would require significant investment and coordination."

Nathaniel nodded thoughtfully. "It could also strengthen Ashcombe's ties with the neighboring estates."

"That's what I was thinking," Eva said, her brow furrowing. "But it's a risk. If something goes wrong, it could strain those relationships instead of solidifying them."

Nathaniel reached out, his hand brushing lightly against hers. "You've never shied away from a challenge, Eva. And you've built Ashcombe into a place that others look to for leadership. Whatever you decide, you'll make it work."

Her chest tightened at the quiet confidence in his voice, and she nodded, her resolve strengthening. "Thank you, Nathaniel. For always believing in me."

"Always," he replied, his gaze steady.

The following weeks were consumed by preparations for the storage project. Eva worked closely with Whitlock and other landowners to draft agreements and allocate resources, her days a blur of meetings, letters, and endless calculations.

Sophia proved invaluable during this time, her charm and strategic mind smoothing over potential conflicts and winning allies where Eva had feared resistance.

"You've got them eating out of the palm of your hand," Sophia said one afternoon as they returned to the manor after a particularly successful meeting.

Eva laughed, shaking her head. "I think that's more your doing than mine."

Sophia grinned, her eyes sparkling. "Maybe. But you're the one they trust, Eva. And that's worth more than charm."

As the project began to take shape, Eva couldn't help but feel a growing sense of satisfaction. The shared storage facilities would not only benefit Ashcombe but also strengthen the bonds between estates, creating a network of support that could weather future challenges.

Nathaniel was a constant presence throughout the process, his practical insights and steady leadership invaluable as they navigated the complexities of the project.

One evening, as they stood together in the northern fields, watching the workers begin construction on the first facility, Nathaniel turned to Eva, his expression thoughtful.

"You've done something incredible here," he said softly. "This project, the northern fields, everything—it's a legacy that will last long after us."

Eva glanced at him, her heart swelling at the warmth in his gaze. "It's our legacy, Nathaniel. None of this would have been possible without you."

His lips curved into a faint smile, and he reached for her hand, his grip warm and reassuring. "And I wouldn't want to be anywhere else."

As summer approached, the project neared completion, its progress a testament to the strength of the community and the partnerships Eva had forged.

The opening ceremony for the first storage facility was held on a bright June morning, the fields around it lush with crops and the air alive with the hum of anticipation.

Eva stood before the gathered crowd, her heart pounding as she addressed them.

"This project is more than just a building," she began, her voice steady despite the weight of the moment. "It's a symbol of what we can achieve when we work together—across estates, across communities. It's a promise of resilience, of hope, and of a future we can all share."

The applause that followed was deafening, and as Eva stepped back, Nathaniel was there to greet her, his smile filled with pride.

"You were brilliant," he said, his voice low.

Eva's cheeks flushed, and she smiled, her heart light. "It's because of everyone here—including you."

That evening, as the celebrations continued and the tenants danced in the village square, Eva and Nathaniel found a quiet moment on the terrace of the manor.

The sun dipped below the horizon, casting the estate in hues of gold and amber, and the soft strains of music drifted up from the square.

"I've been thinking about something," Nathaniel said suddenly, his voice breaking the comfortable silence.

Eva glanced at him, her curiosity piqued. "What is it?"

He turned to face her, his hazel eyes filled with quiet intensity. "I've spent my life looking for a place to belong, Eva. And I've found it here—with you. I want to make that official."

Her breath caught, her heart pounding as he reached into his pocket and pulled out a simple gold ring.

"Eva," he said softly, his voice trembling with emotion. "Will you marry me?"

Tears filled her eyes, and she nodded, her voice barely above a whisper. "Yes, Nathaniel. A thousand times, yes."

As he slipped the ring onto her finger and their lips met in a soft, lingering kiss, Eva felt a quiet certainty settle over her.

Ashcombe's future was bright, its people united, and her heart full. And for the first time, she allowed herself to dream—not just of what was, but of all that could be.

Chapter Forty-Eight

The celebrations for the storage facility's opening continued late into the night, the village square alive with music, dancing, and laughter. For Eva, it was a moment of triumph, but her attention occasionally wandered to her sister, whose sparkling energy had captured the crowd.

Sophia was radiant, her laughter ringing above the hum of conversation as she moved effortlessly among the guests. Her charm was infectious, drawing smiles and attention wherever she went.

"You've got competition," Nathaniel teased, his hazel eyes twinkling as he stood beside Eva near the edge of the square.

Eva followed his gaze to where Sophia was engaged in animated conversation with a tall, dark-haired man in a finely tailored coat.

"Who is that?" Eva asked, her brow furrowing in curiosity.

"Lord Lucien Arborough," Nathaniel replied, his tone thoughtful. "A widower with significant landholdings just south of Whitlock's estate. He's well-respected but keeps to himself."

Eva watched as Lucien leaned in slightly, his expression intent as Sophia laughed at something he said. Her sister's usual playfulness seemed tempered by genuine interest, a rare shift that piqued Eva's curiosity.

Later, as the crowd began to thin and the music softened to a more languid rhythm, Eva found Sophia near the fountain, her cheeks flushed from dancing.

"You seemed to be enjoying yourself," Eva said, her tone light but laced with curiosity.

Sophia grinned, her eyes sparkling. "It was a celebration, wasn't it? Besides, it's not every day I find myself in conversation with someone as intriguing as Lord Arborough."

Eva raised an eyebrow. "Intriguing, is he?"

Sophia's smile widened, but her tone turned uncharacteristically serious. "He's different, Eva. Thoughtful, reserved—but there's a depth to him. He asked about Ashcombe, about you and the tenants. He seems to genuinely care about the things that matter."

Eva's curiosity deepened, and she placed a hand on her sister's arm. "Be careful, Sophia. Men like him don't often wear their intentions plainly."

Sophia nodded, her expression thoughtful. "I know. But for once, I think I'd like to see where this leads."

In the weeks that followed, Lucien's presence at Ashcombe became more frequent. He visited under the guise of discussing the storage facilities and the regional partnership, but it quickly became clear that his interest in Sophia extended far beyond business.

Nathaniel observed the dynamic with quiet amusement, often sharing knowing looks with Eva when Sophia and Lucien were lost in conversation.

"Your sister has met her match," Nathaniel remarked one afternoon as they watched the pair from the terrace.

Eva folded her arms, her gaze steady. "If anyone can keep up with Sophia, it might be him. But I still wonder if he truly understands what he's getting into."

Nathaniel laughed, his voice warm. "He's a quick study, if nothing else. And it's clear he sees something in her that he values."

One evening, as the Arborough carriage rolled down the drive after another visit, Sophia found Eva in the drawing room, her expression unusually introspective.

"Well?" Eva prompted, setting down her embroidery.

Sophia hesitated, then sat beside her sister, her voice uncharacteristically soft. "Lucien asked me to visit his estate. To see how our partnership might evolve."

Eva arched an eyebrow. "And?"

"And," Sophia continued, her cheeks flushing faintly, "I think he's asking for more than a tour."

A silence settled between them before Eva reached out, her tone gentle. "Do you care for him?"

Sophia looked away, her voice trembling slightly. "I think I could. He's patient, kind. And he sees me—not just as the lively younger sister or the charming guest, but as someone who could stand beside him."

Eva's chest tightened, her own memories of finding love coloring her response. "Then follow your heart, Sophia. But remember, you're more than enough as you are. Don't let him—or anyone—dim the light that makes you who you are."

Sophia nodded, her expression filled with quiet determination. "I won't. But, Eva... what if this could be something more?"

"Then you owe it to yourself to find out," Eva replied, her voice steady.

The next few weeks were a flurry of visits between Ashcombe and Arborough's estate. Lucien showed Sophia the lands he had meticulously cared for, sharing stories of his late wife and the years he had spent rebuilding after her loss.

For Sophia, it was a revelation. Lucien's reserved nature masked a profound depth of feeling, and his admiration for her was evident in every word and gesture.

By midsummer, whispers of an engagement began to circulate, though Sophia remained characteristically coy when questioned.

One evening, as the sisters prepared for bed, Sophia finally broached the subject.

"He hasn't asked yet," she admitted, her voice tinged with anticipation. "But I think he will. And, Eva... I think I'll say yes."

Eva smiled, her heart swelling with pride and affection. "Then you'll have my blessing—and all the support you need."

Sophia grinned, her usual playfulness returning. "You'll have to plan the wedding, of course. Someone has to keep the Arborough estate from being overwhelmed by my ideas."

Eva laughed, pulling her sister into a hug. "I wouldn't expect anything less."

Sophia's budding romance with Lucien brought a new dimension to life at Ashcombe. The possibility of a union between their estates hinted at a future filled with collaboration and mutual prosperity—a testament to the bonds that had grown from Ashcombe's transformation.

As Eva watched her sister navigate this new chapter, she couldn't help but feel a sense of wonder at how far they had come.

Ashcombe was thriving, her family was flourishing, and love—unpredictable, transformative, and endlessly inspiring—continued to shape their lives in ways she never could have imagined.

Chapter Forty-Nine

The whispers of Sophia's relationship with Lord Lucien Arborough reached Fairmont's ears sooner than Eva had anticipated. It wasn't long before subtle signs of his discontent began to surface—tenants from neighboring lands reporting increased scrutiny, merchants hinting at new trade restrictions, and veiled threats cloaked in the formalities of correspondence.

But if Fairmont intended to rattle Ashcombe, he would have to try harder.

The morning Lucien arrived at Ashcombe unannounced, Eva was in the northern fields, inspecting the progress of the crops with Nathaniel. A messenger galloped up, his face flushed from the ride.

"Lady Ashcombe," he said, bowing quickly. "Lord Arborough has arrived at the manor and requests a meeting."

Eva exchanged a glance with Nathaniel, her brow furrowing. "Did he say what it was about?"

"No, my lady," the messenger replied. "Only that it was urgent."

Eva nodded, her heart quickening. "Thank you. Tell him I'll be there shortly."

Lucien was waiting in the drawing room, his usually composed demeanor tinged with tension. Sophia stood beside him, her hand resting lightly on his arm, her expression a mix of concern and determination.

"Lucien," Eva said as she entered, her tone warm but questioning. "This is an unexpected visit."

Lucien inclined his head, his dark eyes serious. "My apologies for the abruptness, Lady Ashcombe. But I've received word that Lord Fairmont has been leveraging his connections to undermine the regional partnerships you've worked so hard to build."

Eva's stomach tightened, though she kept her expression calm. "What sort of leverage?"

Lucien reached into his coat and produced a folded letter, handing it to her. "He's been spreading rumors that your irrigation project has caused irreparable damage to neighboring lands. He's urging others to withdraw their support and isolate Ashcombe."

Eva scanned the letter, her jaw tightening. The accusations were false, but Fairmont's influence could make them difficult to disprove in the court of public opinion.

"Why would he go to such lengths?" Sophia asked, her voice tinged with indignation.

"Because he sees Ashcombe's success as a threat," Nathaniel said, entering the room with a purposeful stride. "And he won't stop until he feels secure in his position again."

Lucien nodded, his expression grim. "That's why I'm here. Fairmont may have influence, but he's not invincible. If we combine the strength of Ashcombe and Arborough, we can counter his efforts—and ensure the region sees the truth."

Eva looked up from the letter, her gaze steady. "And what does that partnership look like, Lucien?"

Lucien hesitated, then glanced at Sophia. His expression softened as he took her hand.

"I've come to ask for her hand in marriage," he said simply, his voice filled with quiet conviction.

The room fell silent, the weight of his words settling over them.

"Sophia," Eva said softly, her gaze shifting to her sister. "Is this what you want?"

Sophia's cheeks flushed, but her voice was steady as she replied. "Yes. I care for him, Eva. And I believe in what we can build together."

Eva's chest tightened with a mix of emotions—pride, love, and a lingering protectiveness. She turned back to Lucien, her tone firm. "If this is to happen, it must be for more than strategy. Sophia deserves a life filled with love and respect."

Lucien met her gaze, his voice unwavering. "I would give her nothing less."

Eva nodded slowly, her heart swelling. "Then you have my blessing. And Ashcombe's support."

The announcement of Sophia's engagement to Lord Arborough sent ripples through the region. While many celebrated the union as a symbol of unity and progress, Fairmont's reaction was swift and pointed.

"He'll see this as an escalation," Nathaniel warned one evening as they reviewed correspondence in the study. "Lucien's influence bolsters Ashcombe's position—and Fairmont won't let that go unanswered."

"Let him try," Eva replied, her voice steady. "We've faced his schemes before, and we'll face them again. The difference now is that we're not alone."

The weeks leading up to the wedding were a whirlwind of preparation and intrigue. Sophia and Lucien spent their days planning the ceremony while Eva worked tirelessly to solidify the alliances their union would create.

Fairmont, true to form, attempted to sow discord among the landowners who had supported Ashcombe. But with Lucien's influence and Eva's steadfast leadership, his efforts met resistance.

At the heart of it all, Sophia remained a beacon of light, her infectious laughter and boundless energy lifting the spirits of everyone around her.

"You're not just marrying Lucien," Eva teased one afternoon as they inspected the manor's flower arrangements. "You're marrying into a new world of responsibilities."

Sophia grinned, her eyes sparkling. "And I'll tackle them the way I tackle everything—with style and flair."

Eva laughed, pulling her sister into a hug. "I have no doubt you will."

The wedding was held on a warm summer's day, the ceremony taking place in the gardens of Arborough's estate. Guests from across the region gathered, their presence a testament to the growing power of the Ashcombe-Arborough alliance.

Eva stood beside Sophia as she prepared to walk down the aisle, her sister's usual confidence giving way to a rare vulnerability.

"You'll be magnificent," Eva said softly, squeezing Sophia's hand.

Sophia smiled, her eyes shining with emotion. "Thank you, Eva. For everything."

As Sophia and Lucien exchanged vows, Eva felt a deep sense of pride and hope. Their union was more than a marriage—it was a promise of what could be achieved through love, partnership, and determination.

In the days that followed, Fairmont's influence began to wane as the strength of the Ashcombe-Arborough alliance became clear.

For Eva, the victory was bittersweet. While the threat to Ashcombe had lessened, she knew that challenges would always lie ahead. But as she stood with Nathaniel on the terrace, the estate bathed in the golden light of dusk, she felt ready to face them.

"With you by my side," she said softly, her gaze on the horizon, "there's nothing we can't overcome."

Nathaniel's hand found hers, his grip warm and steady. "Together, Eva. Always."

As the first stars appeared in the night sky, Eva allowed herself to dream—not just of Ashcombe's future, but of the legacy they would leave behind.

The announcement of Sophia's engagement to Lord Lucien Arborough sent waves through the region. For most, it was a cause for celebration—a union that symbolized strength, prosperity, and the promise of collaboration. But for others, particularly Lord Fairmont, it was a declaration of war.

Fairmont's anger came not in loud proclamations but in the quieter, more insidious ways that made him dangerous.

A week after the announcement, Nathaniel entered the manor's study, his expression grim.

"We've received reports from tenants on the southern boundary," he said, handing Eva a folded letter. "Fairmont's men have been harassing travelers, claiming that Ashcombe's trade routes encroach on his land."

Eva's chest tightened as she read the letter. The complaints were familiar—groundless accusations meant to sow doubt and create conflict.

"He's testing us," Eva said, her voice steady but cold. "Trying to see how far he can push before we respond."

Nathaniel leaned against the desk, his brow furrowed. "What's our move?"

Eva set the letter down, her mind racing. "We don't give him what he wants. Send word to Cartwright to investigate quietly. If Fairmont is overstepping, we'll take it to the council—with evidence."

"And if he escalates?" Nathaniel asked.

Eva met his gaze, her resolve hardening. "Then we escalate too."

As tensions simmered, Sophia and Lucien continued their preparations for the wedding, blissfully unaware of the storm brewing around them. But Eva couldn't help noticing the subtle shifts in

Lucien's demeanor—a stiffness in his posture, a guarded edge to his words.

Late one evening, as the sisters sat together in the drawing room, Sophia voiced her own concerns.

"Lucien's been distracted lately," she said, twirling a strand of hair around her finger. "I think Fairmont's interference is weighing on him."

Eva set down her teacup, her brow furrowing. "Have you spoken to him about it?"

Sophia sighed, her usual confidence tempered by uncertainty. "Not directly. I don't want to burden him when he's already dealing with so much."

Eva reached out, placing a hand on her sister's. "Sophia, a marriage is built on trust and partnership. If something is troubling him, you need to face it together."

Sophia nodded slowly, her expression thoughtful. "You're right. I'll talk to him."

The opportunity came sooner than expected. Two days later, Lucien arrived at Ashcombe, his expression tense as he requested a private meeting with Eva and Nathaniel.

In the study, Lucien wasted no time getting to the point.

"Fairmont has sent me a message," he said, placing a folded letter on the desk.

Eva opened it, her stomach tightening as she read the contents. Fairmont's words were thinly veiled threats, accusing Lucien of betraying his peers by aligning with Ashcombe and warning of consequences should the marriage proceed.

"He's trying to isolate you," Nathaniel said, his tone grim.

Lucien nodded, his jaw tightening. "He's already begun pressuring my neighboring estates. They're wary of crossing him, even though they know his claims are baseless."

Eva set the letter down, her mind racing. "He wants to make you doubt the alliance. If he can divide us, he thinks he can weaken us."

Lucien's gaze met hers, his expression resolute. "He underestimates me, as well as you. I won't back down, and I won't abandon Sophia—or Ashcombe."

That evening, as Eva and Nathaniel walked the perimeter of the estate, the weight of the situation settled heavily on her shoulders.

"Fairmont won't stop until he's forced to," Nathaniel said, his voice breaking the silence.

Eva glanced at him, her expression thoughtful. "The question is how far he's willing to go—and how far we're prepared to push back."

Nathaniel's hand brushed against hers, his touch grounding her. "You're not alone in this, Eva. Whatever comes, we face it together."

She nodded, her resolve strengthening. "Then let's make sure Ashcombe is ready."

The days leading up to the wedding were filled with tension as Eva and Nathaniel worked behind the scenes to counter Fairmont's schemes. Cartwright's investigations revealed a pattern of harassment along the southern trade routes, and Eva began compiling the evidence needed to bring the matter to the council.

But even as the preparations for confrontation continued, the estate buzzed with anticipation for the wedding. Sophia's joy was infectious, her excitement a reminder of what they were fighting to protect.

On the eve of the ceremony, Lucien approached Eva in the drawing room, his expression earnest.

"Thank you," he said simply.

Eva tilted her head, her brow furrowing. "For what?"

"For trusting me," Lucien replied. "And for reminding me what's worth fighting for. Fairmont may try to divide us, but he's already lost. The alliances we're building—what Sophia and I are building—are stronger than his influence."

Eva smiled, her chest swelling with pride. "Then let's make sure he understands that."

The wedding was a triumph, the ceremony held in the gardens of Arborough's estate under a brilliant summer sun. Guests from across the region attended, their presence a testament to the strength of the Ashcombe-Arborough alliance.

As Sophia and Lucien exchanged vows, Eva stood with Nathaniel, her heart filled with hope.

"This is more than just a wedding," she said softly. "It's a turning point."

Nathaniel nodded, his hazel eyes steady. "And it's just the beginning."

As they watched the newlyweds walk back down the aisle, hand in hand, Eva felt a quiet certainty settle over her.

Fairmont's shadow still lingered, but the light of Ashcombe's unity and resilience shone brighter. And whatever challenges lay ahead, she knew they would face them together.

Chapter Fifty

The wedding had been a resounding success, but the afterglow of celebration quickly gave way to renewed tensions. Fairmont's reach was longer than Eva had anticipated, and his attempts to disrupt the Ashcombe-Arborough alliance grew increasingly brazen.

Within days of the ceremony, troubling news began to filter in. Merchants who had long traded with Ashcombe reported delays and sudden tariffs, while neighboring estates sympathetic to Fairmont grew less cooperative.

At the heart of it all, however, was a more insidious rumor—a claim that the irrigation system, the very cornerstone of Ashcombe's success, had caused flooding on Fairmont's land.

Late one evening, as rain pattered softly against the windows of the study, Nathaniel entered with a bundle of reports under his arm. His expression was grim.

"It's worse than we thought," he said, setting the papers on the desk. "Fairmont's tenants have started claiming their fields have been waterlogged since we diverted the streams."

Eva's chest tightened as she sifted through the reports. The accusations were false—Ashcombe's irrigation system had been carefully designed to avoid such issues—but the weight of the claims was undeniable.

"He's trying to turn the council against us again," she said, her voice steady despite the storm brewing within her.

Nathaniel nodded. "And he's found sympathetic ears. A hearing has been scheduled for the end of the month."

Eva set the papers down, her jaw tightening. "Then we'll be ready. We've faced his lies before, and we'll face them again."

The weeks leading up to the hearing were a blur of preparation. Eva and Cartwright worked tirelessly to compile evidence disproving Fairmont's claims, while Nathaniel coordinated efforts to shore up Ashcombe's trade routes and maintain morale among the tenants.

Sophia and Lucien, newly returned from their brief honeymoon, threw themselves into the effort as well.

"This isn't just about Ashcombe," Lucien said during a strategy meeting in the manor's library. "It's about the entire region. If Fairmont succeeds in undermining us, he'll only grow bolder."

Sophia leaned forward, her usual levity replaced by a rare seriousness. "Then let's make sure he doesn't succeed."

Eva glanced at her sister, her chest swelling with pride. Sophia's transformation from carefree socialite to determined ally had been a quiet triumph, and her presence was a reminder of how far they had come.

The hearing was held in the council chamber of a nearby town, the same venue where Eva had faced Fairmont's earlier petition. But this time, the stakes felt higher. The rumors of flooding had spread far and wide, and the gallery was filled with curious onlookers eager to see the drama unfold.

Fairmont arrived with his usual air of polished arrogance, his allies flanking him like sentinels. But Eva stood tall, her gaze steady as she entered the chamber with Nathaniel, Lucien, and Cartwright at her side.

The proceedings began with Fairmont's representative presenting their case—a carefully crafted narrative that painted Ashcombe's irrigation project as reckless and self-serving.

Eva listened in silence, her heart pounding but her expression calm. When it was her turn to speak, she rose with quiet confidence, her voice steady as she addressed the council.

"Ladies and gentlemen, the claims brought against Ashcombe are not only false but an insult to the efforts of its people," she began, her gaze sweeping the room. "Our irrigation system was designed with the utmost care, ensuring that the natural flow of water was maintained and that no neighboring lands would be harmed."

She presented maps, engineering plans, and testimony from tenants and workers who had overseen the project. Each piece of evidence was methodically laid out, painting a clear picture of Ashcombe's integrity.

But it was Lucien's testimony that carried the most weight. As a respected landowner with no direct stake in the irrigation system, his words were seen as impartial and authoritative.

"I have walked the fields in question," Lucien said, his voice calm but firm. "And I have found no evidence to support Lord Fairmont's claims. What I have seen, however, is the remarkable transformation of Ashcombe—a testament to innovation and community."

The murmurs that rippled through the gallery were ones of approval, and Eva felt a flicker of hope.

The council's decision came later that afternoon. After hours of deliberation, the lead councilman stood to deliver the verdict.

"The evidence presented by Lady Ashcombe and her representatives is compelling," he said, his voice carrying through the chamber. "It is the opinion of this council that the claims brought by Lord Fairmont are unfounded. Furthermore, we commend Ashcombe for its contributions to the region and encourage other estates to consider similar innovations."

Relief washed over Eva as the gallery erupted into applause. Fairmont's face was a mask of fury as he stormed out of the chamber, his allies trailing behind him.

As they returned to Ashcombe that evening, the mood in the carriage was jubilant. Sophia and Lucien exchanged knowing smiles, while Nathaniel leaned back in his seat, his expression one of quiet satisfaction.

"You were incredible," Nathaniel said softly, his gaze meeting Eva's.

Eva smiled, her heart swelling. "We all were."

Sophia grinned, her usual playfulness returning. "Fairmont never stood a chance—not with this team."

That night, as the estate settled into the quiet rhythms of evening, Eva and Nathaniel stood together on the terrace, the cool breeze carrying the scent of blooming flowers.

"This feels like a turning point," Eva said softly, her gaze on the horizon.

Nathaniel nodded, his hand brushing lightly against hers. "It is. Fairmont's influence is waning, and Ashcombe is stronger than ever."

Eva turned to him, her voice trembling with emotion. "I couldn't have done this without you, Nathaniel. Or without them."

He smiled, his hazel eyes warm. "You've built something remarkable here, Eva. And this is just the beginning."

As their hands intertwined, Eva felt a quiet certainty settle over her. The challenges they had faced were a reminder of the strength that came from unity, and the future stretched out before them—vast, bright, and filled with possibility.

Epilogue

The summer sun bathed Ashcombe in a golden glow, its fields lush with crops that swayed gently in the breeze. The estate hummed with life, a testament to the resilience and unity that had carried it through countless challenges.

Eva stood on the veranda, her gaze sweeping over the land that had come to define her. The sounds of the estate—the chatter of workers, the lowing of cattle, the distant laughter of children—filled her heart with a quiet contentment.

Nathaniel approached from the gardens, a bouquet of freshly cut flowers in his hand.

"For the lady of the manor," he said, his tone teasing as he offered them to her.

Eva laughed softly, accepting the bouquet. "Thank you, Captain Grey. You're as charming as ever."

He grinned, his hazel eyes sparkling. "It's easy to be charming when I have so much to be grateful for."

They stood together in companionable silence, the warmth of his presence grounding her.

Later that afternoon, the family gathered in the shade of the great oak tree near the northern fields. Sophia and Lucien arrived arm in arm, their newlywed glow impossible to miss.

"You've outdone yourself, Eva," Sophia said as she surveyed the picnic spread. "I should leave Arborough's management to Lucien and move back here—it's far more relaxing."

Lucien chuckled, his tone affectionate. "I doubt anyone could stop you if you truly wanted to."

Sophia flashed him a mischievous grin before turning to Eva. "Joking aside, you've built something remarkable. Ashcombe feels like a place where anything is possible."

Eva's chest tightened, her sister's words filling her with pride. "It's because of all of us," she said softly. "This place wouldn't be what it is without the people who believed in it—and in each other."

As the afternoon wore on, the conversation turned to the future. Cartwright, who had joined them for the gathering, shared his thoughts on expanding Ashcombe's trade routes, while Nathaniel floated the idea of hosting a regional forum to share the estate's innovations.

"I think you're on to something," Lucien said, his expression thoughtful. "If we bring together the right minds, we could create a network of estates that supports one another—not just economically, but socially as well."

Eva nodded, her mind already racing with possibilities. "A coalition of sorts," she mused. "It could strengthen the region and give smaller estates a voice they've never had before."

Sophia leaned back against the tree, her smile softening. "Leave it to you two to turn a picnic into a strategy meeting."

The group laughed, but the idea lingered, a spark of inspiration that hinted at what was to come.

That evening, as the sun dipped below the horizon and the first stars appeared in the sky, Eva and Nathaniel returned to the veranda. The estate stretched out before them, its beauty enhanced by the golden hues of dusk.

"Do you ever think about where we started?" Eva asked, her voice quiet.

Nathaniel smiled, his gaze steady. "All the time. And I wouldn't change a thing."

Eva turned to him, her heart full. "Neither would I. This place, these people... they've given me more than I ever thought possible."

"And you've given them the same," Nathaniel replied, his tone filled with quiet conviction.

As their hands intertwined, Eva felt a deep sense of peace settle over her. The journey that had brought her here had been fraught with challenges, but it had also been rich with triumphs, love, and hope.

And as the stars twinkled above Ashcombe, she allowed herself to dream—not just of the legacy they had built, but of the endless possibilities that lay ahead.

Also by Kenneth Thomas

Harrow Harbor Mysteries
Whispering Harbor Mystery
The Secret of the Cavern
The Ghost Ships Shadow

Moonlight Pact series
The Moonlight Pact
The Rift Redemption
The Riftbound Legacy

The Awakening Thread Chronicles
The Awakening Thread

The Broke Kids Club
The Broke Kids Club
The Broke Kids Club: Ripples of Change

The Broke Kids Club Collection
The Broke Kids Club Collection

The Convergence of Minds series
The Digital Agora: A Philosophical Epic of AI and Humanity
Foundation of the Agora
Beyond the Agora: Fractured Realms

The Echoes of Eternity
The Awakening of Nephira
The Rift Of Worlds

The Eclipse Chronicles
Shards of Light
Eclipse Reaver
Axis Reforged

The Veil of Shadows Series
Shattered Dominion
The Fractured Path

Standalone
A Tail of Darkness To Light

The Mirror Within
Echoes of Ink and Heart
Purpose Over Power: The Visionary Path of Servant Leadership
The Questions That Shape Us: Finding Life's Wisdom-The Power of Inquiry
Where the Shadows Settle
30 Days to Inner Freedom: A Mindful Journey in Addiction Recovery
Towards a Sustainable Future: The UN's 17 Goals
Echoes of Becoming
Cognitive Freedom: The Stoic Path to Resilience and Recovery
Beneath the Cypress Sky
The Unbroken Pen
Where Tides Meet
Whispers on Petals

About the Author

Kenneth Thomas is the founder and CEO of Visionary Tide Media, a pioneering company dedicated to creating transformative media and advanced AI solutions. With over two decades of personal experience in addiction recovery, Kenneth brings a unique perspective to his work, blending deep personal insights with professional expertise. His writing covers a broad spectrum, including AI innovation, personal growth, spirituality, and societal improvement, all aimed at making a meaningful impact. Kenneth's commitment to truth, ethics, and the betterment of humanity is evident in his diverse projects, which include published works, media content, and AI-driven initiatives. Through Visionary Tide Media, he aspires to inspire, educate, and elevate his audience, fostering a world enriched by genuine understanding and compassion.